THE LOWLY MAID'S TRIUMPH

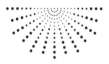

DOLLY PRICE

CONTENTS

Introduction   v

Chapter 1   1
Chapter 2   11
Chapter 3   15
Chapter 4   18
Chapter 5   21
Chapter 6   25
Chapter 7   28
Chapter 8   31
Chapter 9   38
Chapter 10   48
Chapter 11   50
Chapter 12   52
Chapter 13   54
Chapter 14   61
Chapter 15   63
Chapter 16   69
Chapter 17   73
Chapter 18   77
Chapter 19   80
Chapter 20   88
Chapter 21   93
Chapter 22   98
Chapter 23   102
Chapter 24   110
Chapter 25   112
Chapter 26   114
Chapter 27   116
Chapter 28   119
Chapter 29   122
Chapter 30   125
Chapter 31   127
Chapter 32   131

Chapter 33	133
Chapter 34	136
Chapter 35	138
Chapter 36	142
Chapter 37	145
Chapter 38	150
Chapter 39	153
Chapter 40	156
Chapter 41	162
Chapter 42	165
Chapter 43	167
Chapter 44	169
Chapter 45	171
Chapter 46	174
Chapter 47	176
Chapter 48	178
Chapter 49	180
Chapter 50	182
Chapter 51	183
Love Victorian Romance?	187
Our Gift To You	189

INTRODUCTION

A PERSONAL WORD FROM PUREREAD

 Dear reader,

It is our utmost pleasure and privilege to bring these wonderful stories to you. I am so very proud of our amazing team of writers, and the delight they continually bring to us all with their beautiful tales of hope, faith, courage and love.

Only once a story is read does it fulfill it's God given purpose, and that makes you, the dear reader, the key that unlocks the treasures that lay within the pages of this book.

Thank you for choosing PureRead!

A Warm Welcome From Dolly Price

PUREREAD
CLEAN READS
FOR PURE HEARTS

To find out more about PureRead and receive new release information and other goodies from Dolly Price go to our website PureRead.com/dollyprice

* * *

Enjoy The Story!

CHAPTER ONE

1 875

"Our Anna, you are silly an' all! Papa told me how Stevie came!"

"I'm not silly! You're silly! I asked Aunt Maud!"

The voices of the little girls were raised, and both seemed ready to burst into tears.

"Girls, girls, what is the matter?" Their father came thumping down the wooden staircase into the hall. The little girls rushed to him, talking at once.

"Anna says that Baby Stevie was under a cabbage!" cried the eldest, Sandra, with scorn. "And *you* told me that Dr. Howard brought him in his bag!"

"Aunt Maud said Mama found Stee'pee under a cabbage! He was lonely and she brought him in!" cried Anna.

"Oh, I see, I see." Mr. Boone stroked his beard, a little perplexed as to how to get out of the question.

"So, which is it, Papa?" asked Sandra. The eldest at seven years old, she was a little impatient.

Mr. Boone thought for a moment. It had never occurred to him that the manner of the baby's arrival should excite his daughters' curiousity, and that he and Maud should have collaborated on the story had been the furthest thing from his mind.

"We were both right," he conceded at last. "Dr. Howard found him under a cabbage and popped him into his bag and brought him to Mama." It was very lame, he knew, especially for his firstborn, Sandra. Anna, who would turn six in June, was satisfied. But he knew that Sandra believed him not at all. She was staring hard at him with that look in her big green eyes which he had been told were just like his own. His explanation would not do!

"Why was Dr. Howard in our garden?" she asked, perplexed.

Mr. Boone was saved by Aunt Maud bustling along the hallway toward the parlour where she had been giving the children their lessons.

"Oh, there you are," she said a little severely to the children. "I only went away for a moment to get my book, and out you came into the hall, to bother your busy father! You should learn to be quiet and obedient. The de Lacy children are always quiet and obedient. Come along now, time for arithmetic." She ushered the two girls back to the parlour, to their father's relief.

"Really, Henry!" remarked Aunt Maud over her shoulder as she pushed the children ahead of her. "These children have no discipline! And if I were you, I would turn the fourth bedroom into a classroom. I was never in a house where the children roam all over where they like! You and Bella are so bohemian!"

"Oh Maud! A poor simple country farmer like myself can't afford a nursery and maids to run it," replied her younger brother with good humour. They had often had this conversation. Maud had come to help with Mrs. Boone's lying-in by taking care of the older children. She freely shared her opinion on how a house with children should be run. His wife Bella could not stand her, but Henry was too fond of his older sister to discourage her from visiting, especially when she was an able manager and very willing to help.

"Poor and simple!" Maud snorted. "You're one of the first families in Glendale, and you know it! You and Bella are soft in the head." She slammed the door and Mr. Boone heard the loud command to the girls to seat themselves and open their books.

What Maud said was not quite true, yet the Boones were comfortable. A large old sprawling farmhouse, built of stone, on one hundred and twenty acres was his, with hardy Galloway cattle dotting the meadows and hundreds of sheep on the hillsides. Situated five miles north of Skipton near the village of Glendale, the farm was in a sweeping valley of the Yorkshire Dales. Sheltered somewhat by the hills, the winter was not as severe as in other parts, and the hay in summer was plentiful.

Henry Boone was forty years old and had married eight years before. Two girls had been born; and three years ago the heir to the farm had arrived. Little Henry, called Harry, was a robust, sturdy fellow already given to the destruction of everything in sight. His second son Stevie had been born just three days before. He'd had to explain the arrival to the girls but never suspected that they would also ask his sister. Sandra, older and sharper than Anna, hadn't believed a word of his lame explanation. He chuckled to himself. He enjoyed his children. A nursery indeed! Maud had evidently forgotten her own childhood spent running wild in the meadows. She had kept house for him after their parents had died. But being very independent, she hadn't been content to stay on when he married and play second fiddle to the young bride. She'd hand-picked a wealthy family in Newcastle-on-Tyne and offered her services as governess; the joke was that the parents were in mortal fear of her. She had been very liberal with her advice on child rearing ever since.

"Maud," he said putting his head in the door. "It's a summer day; don't keep them cooped up too long." She looked a little cross. "The de Lacys …" she began, but Mr. Boone beat a retreat.

Soon after, the girls tumbled out into the sunshine, with instructions from Aunt Maud to keep their pinafores clean and not to go near the bull or the geese. It was May and the meadows and hedges were bursting with colour. They picked daisies and cowslips and, finding them troublesome to carry after a while, threw them into a shallow stream and watched them float away. They took off their boots and splashed their way through the water, with Sandra holding Anna's hand. With bare feet they took off toward a field, clambering over one of the many old walls. Polly, a placid cow and a favourite of theirs, allowed them to pet her calf. A threatening cloud caused them to race to the field barn where they took shelter. Roaming on, they ducked through a hogget hole and were instantly in the midst of a flock of sheep. They gambolled with the lambs. Sandra and Anne scampered to all their favourite places, ending up at the paddock to watch the young foal gallop around on long spindly legs, his mother turning her head every few moments to keep an eye on him in between chomping mouthfuls of green grass. After they had tired of that, they ran back to the stream to retrieve their stockings and boots, with Sandra helping her little sister with hers. They went to the orchard and climbed a little way up a gnarled tree and Sandra told Anna the story of *Little Ida*, whose flowers drooped, but Anna, a sensitive child, cried for the flowers they had thrown into the stream, so Sandra suggested they go and see Old Sal in the poultry yard.

Old Sal, as most people called her, was not really old at all, but her lined face and wispy white hair made her appear so. She had a marked stoop from bending over her charges to feed, admonish, and keep order. Her duties were light; she collected the eggs in the mornings from various locations, fed her flock; watched the little chicks thrive and locked her feathered friends up for the night, safe from foxes. The rooster, Napoleon, was a strutting old bird, cranky, with a large red comb; the children were afraid of him, but Old Sal kept him in his place, and they were quite safe. But the geese! The gander, especially, was fierce. Even the sheepdogs gave Ivan the Terrible, the name bestowed on him by their father, a wide berth. Now he was leading his flock in some adventure of their own to the other side of the farmyard, and they made a terrific noise altogether.

"Any news, Sal?" asked Sandra with eagerness. She was their favourite servant.

"Well let's see now—see our Veronica there?" Sal pointed a bony finger at a young pullet with gleaming red feathers who walked daintily about the yard. "She's been naughty, pushing poor Miss Nightingale out of th'way this mornin' cos there was a piece of toast she fancied that Miss Nightingale got to first, and our Miss Nightingale nearly fell over, and made a noisy squawking too."

"Was she hurt?" exclaimed Anna with anxiety.

"Oh no, not hurt, just cross, she went after our Veronica, but that young 'un's agile, and up she goes on wall, flapping 'er

5

wings. And while Miss Nightingale was chasing our Veronica, our Loretta came over fast as lightening and took th' piece o'toast and off she goes over there, to corner, to peck in peace. It's time for me to 'ave my cup o'tea now, Misses, so I'm off to kitchen. Why don't you come in too, and Mrs. Wall will give you scones, for she was a-bakin' of them this afternoon. I smell them this far away, don't you?"

The girls suddenly realised how hungry they were, and they skipped alongside Old Sal to the kitchen, where they were bidden to sit at the long white table. Hot scones, dripping with butter and raspberry jam, were set in front of them and washed down with cups of milk. As they were eating, Aunt Maud came in. Both girls slunk down in their chairs so that she would not notice their soiled clothes with those beady eyes that darted from place to place, missing nothing.

"There you are!" she said severely. "What kept you so long? Mrs. Wall, I don't want them to eat before their supper. It will spoil their appetites."

"Mrs. Boone says it is all right," said Mrs. Wall with resignation. Mrs. Boone was no great shakes as a mother, in her opinion. She was very lackadaisical. Miss Boone, she had known all her life. She was a small, hardy one, but honest and always said what was on her mind.

Old Sal, sitting in her usual spot at the table, the place reserved for the lowest servant, smiled an almost toothless smile at Miss Boone. She had watched her grow up from a baby. Old Sal had spent all her life in a small cabin not far away from the poultry she tended. She had suffered violent seizures as a child and after she'd recovered, had only been able to learn simple tasks. Her knowledge of her poultry, and the personalities of her charges, though, was beyond anyone's. Miss Boone had always been good to her.

"Sal, it's good to see you again. Are you well?" Aunt Maud's features softened. Sandra thought Aunt Maud was nicer when she smiled. Why didn't she smile more often?

"I'm going on very well, Miss." Old Sal replied. She had a little shake in her hand and her cup rattled in its saucer as the tea spilled over the top.

"I just made a pot of tea, Miss Boone." Mrs. Wall said. "Would you like a cup sent up to parlour? I sent some up to the Mistress."

"Tea? Won't that keep the baby awake all night?" exclaimed Maud, whose knowledge of infant feeding outside of lambs and calves was non-existent. "And don't stand on ceremony with me, Mrs. Wall. I'll drink it here." There was a scraping on the flagstones as she pulled out a chair and sat down. Unconcerned about spoiling her own appetite, she ate two scones with butter, cream, and jam.

"Let's go and see Mamma now!" Sandra said after Aunt Maud had left the kitchen, and they were soon flying up the old wooden staircase in stockinged feet to their mother's room.

Mrs. Boone was a very pretty woman fourteen years younger than her husband. She had been a town girl from Nottingham, and, while she loved her farmer, the work expected of a farmer's wife was quite beyond her. But Mrs. Wall, who not only cooked but kept house with the help of a maid-of-all-work, Joanie, was an able manager.

Bella had met Henry Boone at the wedding of a mutual friend. As she'd danced with him, she'd become attracted to his twinkling green eyes, and she was sure that hard work on a farm must have given him more strength and vigour than city men. She had immediately lost interest in city men. Attorneys and accountants seemed suddenly weak and spineless compared to this handsome, rugged man down from Yorkshire. He had contrived to visit Nottingham several times and they had fallen in love. Her parents had not been pleased but had not stood in her way. She knew that the servants would have preferred a mistress born to the life, so to compensate she was lenient and did not interfere. She brought her personal maid, Jenkins, from Nottingham. Henry, who had persuaded Mr. Harvey that he'd be able to keep his daughter *'in the style to which she was accustomed'* had made no objection. Jenkins kept her clothes in excellent condition and was an elegant hairdresser, so that whenever Mrs. Boone appeared in public, she was looked at and envied by the other farmers' wives, many of whom had neither money nor time to spend on themselves.

Maud thought Bella vain and spoilt; she was not at all the sort of wife for Glendale Farm; Bella's opinion of her sister-in-law was that she was brash and unfeminine. Not until Maud left, six months after Bella entered the house, did she realise how much work she did—housekeeping, cheesemaking, curing, baking, even wringing the wash, sweeping, and other menial tasks—whatever was to be done, if no servant was to hand, Maud got down to it. Bella fully intended to learn some skills, but by then she was expecting a baby, and it would have to wait, but apart from learning how to hand-feed motherless lambs she'd never got around to it. Now she had given her husband four healthy children, and she was very proud of that.

Mrs. Boone was sitting up in bed on several pillows and received her girls with affectionate smiles. She noted the grubby pinafores, feeling a certain quiet satisfaction that Maud would be angry about it. After looking with interest at Stevie in his cradle, Anna jumped up on the bed and snuggled up to her, while Sandra sat on the edge. Both girls loved their pretty Mamma whose thick golden hair fell in long swirls and curls on her bosom. She appeared to be delicate and beautiful, she wore violets or pinks and a sweet scent of roses always hovered about her. Both girls wanted to be just like her when they were grown up. Sandra, however, felt that Anna was more like their mother than she was, and this made her a little jealous of her sister. She wished she had beautiful hair like her Mamma and Anna, but hers was brown—*a bit mousey*, she had heard Mamma tell Jenkins, when she thought she wasn't there, as if sad about it.

Anna was stroking the sleeves of her mamma's frilly shell-pink combing jacket.

"I don't like Aunt Maud," she confided in a whisper, cupping her hand over her mouth against her mother's ear.

"Oh dear, you mustn't say that," said her mother, but she giggled like a naughty child. She held out her other arm toward her older daughter. "Come here, Sandra!" she said, half encouragement, half-reproof. Sandra obeyed very willingly and came into her mother's embrace but could not really understand why she could not be like Anna, who melted naturally into her mother's arms whenever they were together. But with her mother now stroking her hair, mousey as it was, she was happy.

Bella hid her continual regret that Sandra was distant with her. She felt blamed in some way, by her, even though Sandra had been far too young to understand and had no memories of her first year. Her grandmother, Mrs. Harvey, had come to attend the birth. Everything had gone well, and Dr. Howard had departed leaving mother and baby, as he thought, in good hands. Mrs. Harvey had persuaded her daughter that she could not possibly be expected to feed the baby herself. She was too refined and had too nervous a disposition to make a go of it, whereas lower-class women took greatly to it. She herself had sent all of her own children out. Mrs.

Harvey had already made the necessary enquiries, and the new baby, on a bitter December day, was sent to a cottager's wife in Glendale, named Mrs. Giles, who had a baby of six months. Mr. Boone, who had been out in the fields all day from early morning tending the stock, came in that night to find his daughter gone and his wife in floods of regretful tears. He had been furious. He and his mother-in-law had a big quarrel. Bella begged him to go and fetch Sandra first thing in the morning.

But the following days brought heavy snowfalls which made travel impossible for a week. By then, it was too late. Her milk was gone, and Sandra was thriving with Mrs. Giles.

She visited her baby a few times a week, but it had hurt her that, when she'd brought her home at ten months old, Sandra had not settled in well at first. By then, she knew she was to have another baby. Bella was more resolute this time and her mother's attempts to send Anna out were thwarted.

CHAPTER TWO

1
877

"Which is it to be, Bella? School or a governess for the girls?"

It was wintertime two and a half years later, the gas lamp flickered in the draught that blew in the cracks of the old doors and window frames. Mrs. Boone sat by a blazing fire in the cosy parlour, reading a book. The wind blew around the house, but lost in the delightful American novel, *Little Women*, the house could have blown down around her ears.

"They can read quite well, Henry," she replied, her eyes not leaving her book. "And I'm going to read this with them—it's charming! I don't want the girls to go to school. Did we not read *Jane Eyre*? I dread the thought of their meeting a cruel teacher. Anna is very sensitive."

"But Sandra would benefit. She's quick and thinks more like an adult sometimes." Mr. Boone privately thought that sometimes he got more sense out of his nine-year old daughter than he did from his wife. She considered matters before she spoke, and showed promise of good sense. He often asked her opinion about how many more cattle to buy and whether they should breed more Swaledales or Dalesbred sheep. Her answers gave him an opportunity to teach her, and she listened intently. She liked being in his offices, those buildings attached to their house, on paydays. She helped him count out the wages and separate the cash into little piles. He supposed Sandra would continue to help him until Harry was old enough to understand farming matters, though he could already identify different breeds of sheep and cattle and begged to be allowed to shear sheep.

"Jenkins gave notice." Mrs. Boone said, setting aside her book.

"What, she's going back to the city, then? Is she bored here?"

"I think it's because I asked her to mend some of the children's clothes. She hasn't enough to do, with me, I'm not half as vain as I used to be; an old married woman hasn't time, has she? I'm not going to advertise for another lady's maid. It's time we had a nursemaid, though."

"Whatever you think, Bella. With four little ones, you need the help. As long as you don't want to shut them all away in an attic-room, keeping them squeaky-clean all day. Farming children have to pull their weight."

"And how they love being outside, Henry! I do wish I'd been born to this life. I don't think you knew you were taking on such a vain, nervous young lady. Have I improved, do you think?"

"Yes, my love. You have. And you're not half as afeard of the cows, are you?"

"I can still be nervous of a kick. I wish I weren't always thinking of how things can go wrong."

"You do get over anxious at times, Bella."

"But I have you to reassure me," she smiled at him, and held out her hand for his.

Just then a sudden gust of wind shook the old house, and Henry drew closer to the fire.

"Henry, you're shivering! Are you unwell?"

"I've been a bit poorly all day."

"You were out watering the stock, weren't you? I do wish you'd build a big barn for them near the house and save yourself tramping through wet muck every morning and evening. Or at least, why can't you leave these tasks to the labourers?"

"I'm the farmer, I'll do it. The hired hands don't care for them as I do. Like in the Gospel, you know? They'll run if the wolves come."

"There are no wolves anymore, silly man. But I know what you mean. Let me make you a hot cordial, then." Mrs. Boone closed her book and rose.

"Never mind your fruit and berry potions—a hot Scotch, with sugar."

She placed her hand on his forehead.

"Henry! You're burning up! Go to bed immediately, I'll bring you the hot drink."

Her heart being faster than usual, she went downstairs to the kitchen by the light of a gas lamp. She always had a fear that Henry might die and leave her to bring up their children, and there was another on the way. It had happened her aunt, who had never known a moment's ease and comfort afterwards.

She hurried upstairs with the hot punch and watched Henry drink it.

"Stop worrying, Bella," he said. "I will be better tomorrow."

"You must stay in bed tomorrow. The weather will be as bad as today."

"My joints are aching something terrible," he murmured, tossing a little after he had handed her back the glass, turning on his side and back again on to his back. "I've never felt anything like this before."

"Should I call for someone to go for the doctor?" she asked, panic in her voice.

"No, no! Wait until morning! For goodness' sake, Bella, stop worrying!" Henry sounded irritable. He lay back on the pillow and closed his eyes. He got colds every winter, but this was more. It wasn't even influenza, for he had neither sniffle nor cough. He had never felt so ill in his life as he did this night. He was cold and shivering and felt he could not get warm.

"Oh, morning, hurry up!" he heard Bella cry as she hurried from the room. He wished Maud was around; she'd take over in any crisis. But Maud was in Paris. She had left the de Lacys after a disagreement with her mistress, and found an English family leaving for France who needed a strong hand with their boys. She wrote letters full of praise for the Garnets; the boys had reformed from wild animals to tame pets.

CHAPTER THREE

Ben, the senior labourer, was the first employee to appear in the kitchen for an early cup of tea, and Mrs. Boone, who had not slept a wink beside her groaning husband, sent him immediately for the doctor. Dr. Howard came on horseback a short time later and examined his patient with thoroughness. She hovered outside the door, her fingers pressed against her mouth, her eyes large in fear, afraid to enter. The girls already knew that Papa was poorly and Anna, as always the reflection of her mother's feelings, was sobbing. Sandra bit back her tears. Harry and Stevie were kept in the kitchen by Mrs. Wall. But her mother trembled, and that made Sandra frightened as well. What if Papa should die?

The doctor came out of the room then, and motioned that he wished to speak to Mrs. Boone alone, but she grasped Sandra's hand firmly, and sending Anna also to Mrs. Wall, half-dragged her eldest daughter downstairs to the parlour where the discussion would take place.

"Your husband has rheumatic fever," began Dr. Howard. "It's usually seen in persons younger than he, but not always. It is a serious illness—" at these words, Mrs. Boone cried out. "—but far from being a desperate case, Mrs. Boone." he hastened then to say. "He will recover. He must have absolute rest for six weeks. An Invalid Diet, consisting of light, nourishing food, as much as he wishes. Absolute quiet and he is to get no news of anything that would cause him distress of any kind. Are you feeling all right, Mrs. Boone?"

"Yes, Doctor," she said faintly, though she looked far from it, her hand on the back of a chair to steady herself.

"You should consider employing a nurse," the doctor said, looking at her thoughtfully.

"But I can nurse Papa." Sandra spoke up then.

He smiled down at her.

"I'm sure you can, Miss Boone. You would, I am sure make a great nurse." He patted her on the head. "However, one of Miss Nightingale's trained nurses should be employed. Mrs. Boone, I can put you in touch with a Miss Charlton."

"Miss Nightingale's nurses?" Sandra felt puzzled—for she thought immediately of Old Sal and the hen, before she realised that Old Sal had named the hen for Miss Nightingale, whoever she was!

"Can you send her up immediately?" asked her mother, in a faint voice.

"This very day, Mrs. Boone. I will give her some new prescriptions to bring with her. I have already bled him and given him some salicylate acid, which is the usual treatment in these cases. How soon it will bring him relief, I cannot say. I will visit tomorrow."

Mrs. Boone had other questions, such as if he should be told, to which the doctor replied that he had already informed her husband of the diagnosis and that the children could go into the room but they were not to climb on the bed and not hug or kiss their father.

"Doctor, I am *enceinte* again," she said then. "Is there any danger …?"

Sandra did not know what *enceinte* meant and looked with a puzzled frown at her mother.

"No danger," he replied in a soothing tone. "But you must sleep apart from him for now. And you should rest also. For your sake and for the sake of the baby. When are you due? You're not showing yet."

Another baby! Of course Sandra knew by now, from seeing the animals on the farm, where babies came from! Tales of cabbages and doctor's bags had been long discarded. But Mrs. Boone realised what she had said with her daughter in the room and gave an embarrassed little smile.

"Early summer." she said.

The doctor made his farewells, and Sandra, the coming baby forgotten momentarily in her wish to see her father, ran upstairs, but not before an admonition from Mamma not to tell Papa, or anybody yet.

CHAPTER FOUR

S andra saw that her father was not at all comfortable. He was too warm, and yet, if he threw the covers off, he was cold. He tossed and turned. The curtains were drawn to prevent light from disturbing him.

"Papa," she said to him with gentle urgency. "Shall I ask Ben to go to the barns?" The stock were in their field barns for the cold weather, but needed to be watered morning and evening.

"Goodness me, girl, yes. Oh, and tomorrow is Pay-Day. I will have to get up for that."

"No, Papa. The doctor says you can't. I can do it. I know how. Just give me the key to the cash-box."

"You're very capable, Sandra, but too young yet. I can't allow it."

Sandra argued for a time with him, insisting he would not be well enough. She knew she had been successful when he sighed and said:

"Very well. It won't be me, then. Get me a pen and paper, and I'll write a note to Mr. Barraclough to come over and pay the men tomorrow. I'm sure he'll oblige."

Mr. Barraclough's Georgian mansion was a few miles away in the Skipton direction. He was a gentleman farmer—another old family in the area. Some years older than Henry Boone, Mr. Barraclough and Henry often visited each other, exchanging news about markets and prices and animal health matters.

Mr. Boone struggled to sit up in bed, but sank back in defeat upon the damp pillows. His hair fell in wet locks upon his brow.

"It's no good, Sandra, I feel too ill to even hold a pen. Call your mother up here. What is she doing, anyway?" her father sounded querulous.

"I don't know. Probably tending to Stevie."

Her father muttered something inaudible.

Sandra sped downstairs. Her mother was in the parlour, resting beside the fire, her face pale, her eyes closed.

Sandra delivered her message.

"Papa will be ill for weeks, Sandra. I don't know how to manage the farm and the men. I often told your father he should get a steward, but he never listened to me."

"I will help you, Mamma." Sandra said solemnly. "I promise. But Mamma, Papa's sheets and pillows are damp, and he must be very uncomfortable lying in them."

"The nurse will be here soon. She will change them." Her mother placed a hand on her brow. "I have to take a powder. Headaches are not good for me or the baby."

Sandra felt a little angry. It could be hours before Nurse Charlton came.

"Mamma, I can change them, with Joanie."

"Very well, Sandra. Thank you." Her mother rose from the chair and went to her bureau, opening it to take out a pen and paper. "I had better go up and see what he wishes me to write to Mr. Barraclough. I'm filled with dread, Sandra, I don't mind admitting it to you—you heard the doctor. Mark my words, our lives will never be the same again from this day."

Sandra thought her mother exaggerated. Papa was not going to die and that was the most important thing in all this.

CHAPTER FIVE

N urse Charlton stayed three weeks, occupying Aunt Maud's old room. By then, Aunt Maud had got word of her brother's illness and immediately obtained a leave from the Garnets. She wrote from Cherbourg to say that she was upon her way.

Mrs. Boone was sorry to see Nurse Charlton go, for while she had been in the house, she could sleep with ease. Dr. Howard was expressing concern that Mr. Boone was not progressing as quickly as he would like him to.

The day that Mrs. Boone learned that her husband's heart had been damaged by the illness was a day she would never forget. Dr. Howard had again drawn her aside for a conference, and told her to prepare herself. Sandra was again present. The doctor saw her stoicism and was quite frank in her presence, for he realised that she was made of sterner stuff than her mother. It was a pity, he thought, that she had to grow up so fast—many children were kept in happy ignorance of illness in the family until it was absolutely necessary to tell them. But then, many of his poorer patients, in those wretched cottages in the alleys behind the main streets of Skipton, Primrose, Daisy and Bluebell Lanes—had no such luxury. Those children knew all, for many impoverished families lived in one room. Sandra drank in every detail and he saw understanding grow in her wide eyes. She was a steady, sensible girl; and as she seemed to have the maturity of someone older than her years, he treated her almost like another adult. She too asked questions, such as, would their father ever be able to run the farm again?

It was a very good question.

"He will need more help," was the reply. "Does he have a steward?"

Sandra shook her head. Her mother was seated by the window, shocked into distressed silence.

"He should employ a steward. For, Miss Boone, there will be days when he feels well enough to go down to the offices and give the orders, run his accounts and pay the wages, but on other days, it will be impossible. He will be unable to do more than come downstairs for his meals, and after that, rest by the fire for the remainder of the day."

"What about going out to the stock?" Sandra asked faintly.

"Not for a long time." Dr. Howard was grave. "And then for short periods only."

"But the lambing—" Sandra's words died on her lips. The men would have to manage.

Mrs. Boone choked back sobs.

"Your sister-in-law will be here soon," Dr. Howard said kindly to her. "Thank God to have family who are willing and able to come to the rescue. You must be brave, Mrs. Boone!"

"Yes, thank you, Doctor," she said with suppressed sniffles, trying to control herself. Sandra felt distressed for her. But even more distressed for her father. What was he going to do, and how would he react to not being able to go outside for weeks, or perhaps months?

Mr. Boone was most unhappy at the thought. He called the men up to his room and gave them orders. Ben was to be in charge of the others for now. But would the men care for the livestock as he did? Would they notice a cow who was lame, or a sheep who looked poorly?

When Mr. Barraclough had visited and urged him to employ a steward, he reluctantly admitted that this was the only way to keep his farm running. None of the boys working for him had the education or the experience he felt they needed. Certainly, none could handle large sums of money, manage the buying and selling at markets and fairs, deal with the bank in Skipton, or do the accounts.

Mr. Barraclough promised that he would advertise about the farming community around Skipton. But three weeks later, he visited him with hopeful news. His own cousin, Mr. Alfred Craven, was seeking employment. Mr. Craven was thirty-five years old, a single man, who had been brought up on a farm of three hundred acres in Wiltshire but as a younger son, had to make his own way in the world. He had a great head for numbers and in his youth had a bit of wanderlust, and had managed the affairs of several wealthy English families on the Continent. He had been all over Europe and was now tired of travelling and anxious to settle in England.

"I've had a letter from him only this morning," Mr. Barraclough exulted to Mr. Boone, waving the sheet about. "He asks me to look around for a suitable situation for him. What do you think, Boone? I have only heard the best accounts of his business acumen and abilities, and as he's from a farming background, he may just be the person you need."

"He sounds most suitable, Henry!" cried Bella, who was sitting with them in the bedroom, as Sandra was. She was party to every discussion now. "And known to you too, Mr. Barraclough! There could not be a higher recommendation!"

Henry considered for just a few minutes. It would not be easy to find somebody with those qualifications: the farming experience and the knowledge of business.

"Very well," he said at last. "You may write back to Mr. Craven, Barraclough, and tell him that he may apply for a situation here. If he is interested, he can write to me and we can discuss terms."

Sandra thought that after that, her father rested more easily, and her mother was happier. Mr. Barraclough was to write to Mr. Craven straightaway, and it was possible that Mr. Craven might be with them in a few weeks.

CHAPTER SIX

Maud arrived one morning in a donkey-cart, and from the time she entered the house, took over the running of it.

"You do look tired, Bella," she stated not unkindly, throwing off her coat and hat and flinging them on the hall-stand.

"I am excessively fatigued. The doctor said I am to rest, but it is impossible!"

"Everything will be all right now," Maud said with crispness. "Just leave it all to me. And Sandra will help," she added, spying her niece coming into the hall to greet her. She gave her a quick embrace, told her she'd grown and then bounded upstairs, saying that she wished to "see my brother without delay, and find out what I can do for him."

It turned out that there was a great deal she could do. She rode out to the fields and meadows and returned with reports of sicknesses and ailments of several animals, which had been neglected. The labourers were afraid of her and dreaded her approaching them, for her darting eyes missed nothing. She took the ledgers and pored over them, making notes. She had a suspicious nature and trusted nobody, not even Mr. Barraclough. How well did Mr. Barraclough know this cousin of his? She put the question to the man himself. Mr. Barraclough admitted that he hadn't seen him in fifteen years or thereabouts, but his family was sound. He was quite affronted with Miss Boone's probing, and Henry asked her to please stop her enquiries. She could vet him for herself after he arrived, for he had accepted the position, agreed to the terms, and after he had visited some relations and friends he had not seen for years, would be upon his way to Glendale Farm.

Maud took Sandra with her everywhere, and she too learned. She was surprised that she got on very well with Aunt Maud, and it was refreshing to have an adult who would take the reins. Sandra realised that she'd been carrying a burden, a burden that her mother should have been able to bear but could not. In fact, her mother felt like a burden also. She began to admire Aunt Maud but began to see her mother in the same light as Maud saw her—nervous, incapable, and even selfish. She didn't like herself for thinking like this about her own mother, but once it had taken root, she found she could not shake it off.

News of Mr. Boone's illness spread to far-flung members of his own family, and a Mr. and Mrs. Knightley took the train from their home in the south of England to visit him. They were young and warm-hearted and brought gifts for the children. They declined to stay in the house, as they felt it too much trouble for the family, so they stayed at an Inn in Glendale and Mr. Boone provided his carriage for their use, for nobody else needed it. Mrs. Boone and Mrs. Knightley liked each other a great deal.

"I hope to have a family just like yours, one day." said Mrs. Knightley to her, as Stevie, nearly three, napped on her lap, his thumb in his mouth. "But after five years … I am beginning to lose hope."

"But you're still young!" protested Mrs. Boone. "You have many years ahead of you. Tell me, what is your new house in Hove like? I hope I shall see it someday!" The Knightleys had just bought a large house in the very fashionable resort in Sussex.

They left after several days, and the women promised to write to each other.

CHAPTER SEVEN

"Oh, my goodness!" Maud, hardly pausing to swallow her toast before she spoke, had just read a letter from France.

"What is it?" Mrs. Boone was hoping that Maud had lost her position and would stay longer. She had, of necessity, come to regard her as indispensable. The house was clean, the wood floors shining with polish, the carpets beaten to within an inch of their lives; there was cheese and butter every day and the animals had been dosed with every possible prescription under the sun for a great variety of ailments.

"The Garnets are off to Russia, and say that if I am to accompany them, I am to be in Paris by—the 30th of this month!"

"And—are you going? Not to Russia, surely! Russia, of all places!" cried Bella.

"Yes, Russia! Russia!" Maud nodded so vigorously that her head bobbed up and down, causing little Anna to giggle, glancing at Sandra, who was trying not to laugh. Maud's eyes were jumping like two little balls. "They mentioned it, some months ago, and I thought then it was not to happen at all, but now, here it is again, Russia! How I long to go! I shall go!"

"But we need you here," said Bella plaintively. "Henry can't do without you!"

"He has Mr. Craven coming, has he not? What use will I be, with a steward here? We would quarrel, I know. I quarrel with everybody."

"I need you, in the house. Mrs. Wall and Joanie cannot manage it all. And with another baby coming—"

"Fiddlesticks! Sandra can keep house as well as me."

Sandra blushed with the compliment. It wasn't true of course, and yet, Maud had introduced her to the essentials of housekeeping. She had learned how to bake bread. She had churned butter and made cheese. She'd plucked a goose with Old Sal, cleaned it out with Joanie, and stuffed and roasted it with Mrs. Wall. She'd made soap for the laundry and wax for the floor. She'd used the heavy flatiron on sheets ten times larger than herself and folded them into perfect rectangles. Aunt Maud had kept her very, very busy indeed, had been generous with orders but sparse with compliments, but had just said she could run the house. She felt very pleased.

And so Aunt Maud departed the following day, having telegraphed the Garnets. Henry came downstairs to wave her goodbye. He put an arm about his wife. "You see, I'm getting better. Everything is looking up." The steward would be along this week—Mr. Barraclough was not quite certain as to the day.

"I will write to you!" were her parting words as Ben drove her in the carriage from the front door where they waved her off. Nobody knew that her very first letter would go unread and unheeded, and if it had been otherwise, the greatest disaster to ever befall the Boone family could have been averted.

Mr. Barraclough visited that very evening, bringing with him his cousin, their new steward, Mr. Alfred Craven.

CHAPTER EIGHT

He was an affable, rather self-effacing man, with dark hair, a narrow face and thin build, a man who one would expect to have more to say of his travels other than that he liked the Swiss Alps and disliked the heat in Southern Italy. But perhaps he was tired of telling everybody about them. He was very glad to be home in England and grateful for the position, had a great deal of questions about the livestock and the running of Glendale Farm. He certainly knew what he was talking about and the impression he made on the Boones was very favourable. He was staying with the Barracloughs for now; he would need to move to a house on the farm, and there was an old gate-lodge, left over from the days when the farm had been an estate, that could be fitted up for him within the month. He would return on the morrow for a long discourse with Mr. Boone, an introduction to the offices—now to become his offices—and a tour of the farm on horseback conducted by Ben.

"The gate-lodge!" exclaimed Mrs. Boone after they had bid goodbye. "And, are we to bear the expense of fitting it up?"

"Yes, I'm afraid we are."

"And his pay from now on—it will be quite a drain, Henry!"

"Is it only now that occurs to you?" Mr. Boone snapped back. It had been a long day and he felt very tired. His incapacity had hit home today. Sandra saw his fatigue and sadness. Why did such a bad thing have to happen to them? Why did Papa have to become ill and unable to work, making him impatient with Mamma, and even cross sometimes with the little ones? He was rarely cross with her.

"Mr. Craven does this." giggled Anna quietly to Sandra. She threw her face a little upwards and to the side. "Did you see him? He did it lots of times!"

Sandra laughed.

"Girls! Don't be unkind!" their mother said.

The next few days were busy. Mrs. Boone was in the parlour, sitting at her bureau, drawing up a list of items needed to be purchased for the lodge, and was very annoyed at the expense required, not just for their new steward, but also for the servant he would require. When the post was brought in, it contained two letters, one from Mrs. Knightley, which she opened immediately. It was, as usual, warm and full of concern for her and for everybody. The other was only a thin letter in Maud's hand, posted before she had left England. She sighed. She disliked Maud's letters—they made her feel tired. Maud wrote as she did everything—quickly and without pause. This probably contained a hundred instructions that she'd meant to give to her. And why had she written so soon? She shoved the letter in the bureau drawer and decided to leave it until later to give to Henry. But she forgot, and there the letter remained.

Mr. Craven settled in. He grasped the business with ease. He made good bargains at the markets, even better than Mr. Boone had. He showed acumen and saved money with several changes he implemented. The family was so delighted with him that they showered thanks upon Mr. and Mrs. Barraclough and held a dinner party for them, to which they invited their clergyman, Mr. Marsden, and his wife and a few others—to whom they thought he might like to be introduced.

Sandra was very happy to see that her father's mood had improved greatly, and as the weather became better, he began to venture outside. The sunshine and fresh air did everybody good. Mrs. Boone also became happier. Sandra kept house, and even held the keys to the stores. She was busy from dawn to dusk on most days as her mother's time neared. In June, during the haymaking, they welcomed another boy, John Terence.

With her father on the mend, and her mother happy and well, and the joy of a little baby in the house once more, only one thing marred Sandra's happiness, and that was to do with Mr. Craven. She'd been out one day looking at the poultry, chatting to the old woman as usual, when Old Sal's attention was turned to something or somebody in her vision, and her eyes grew large in foreboding. Sandra followed her gaze. Mr. Craven was crossing the farmyard. He took no notice of them and entered the stables.

"What's the matter, Sal?" asked Sandra. But the old woman did not want to tell her. But Sandra persisted. Finally, she said: "Oh Miss Sandra, if there's talk of putting me out, will you speak for me?"

"Putting you out, Sal, what are you talking about?" Sandra was aghast. It was well known that her grandfather had promised Sal's father that there would always be a place for her on the farm. Always.

"I would have to go to workhouse; I don't want to go to workhouse! Will you speak for me, Miss Sandra, will you?" Old Sal burst into tears.

The truth dawned upon Sandra—or at least part of it.

"Oh, Sal. Don't worry. Mr. Craven isn't going to dismiss anybody. He would have to ask Papa first, and Papa would never agree!"

"He come to me and asked me what I do. I told him, and he said nowt. I knows what he is thinking, Miss Sandra, that I'm a waste. Joanie could do this job, or you, or Anna. If I lose my place, I'll have to go to workhouse, Miss Sandra!"

"That will never happen!" Sandra said with conviction. "He was just getting to know everybody who works here!"

"But you will speak for me, will you, Miss Sandra?" Sal gripped her arm with bony fingers.

"Of course, of course! Oh, I do wish you weren't upset, Sal! He didn't mean anything by it. But I'll tell you what—I will have a word with Father. Just in case."

Later, Mr. Boone listened attentively. "He did mention it to me, you know, that her services were in excess of our needs. When he heard the particular circumstances—the promise I made to her father and so on, he understood perfectly and was very sorry he mentioned it. Old Sal shouldn't have taken alarm. She is a—simpleton, and I mean that in the medical sense, that she has limited understanding of the world. She is to be pitied."

"Yes, Papa. She is very frightened of the workhouse."

"Oh, the poor woman. But be reassured, Sandra, she stays. Even when she gets to be beyond working. She has her little cabin here until she dies, and her keep. Now, I have to sleep for a bit. Will you see I'm not disturbed? I did too much yesterday, I think."

Sandra skipped away to reassure Old Sal. It was Friday, and she met her coming out of the office. But Sal was upset. She held her little money-pouch to her chest.

"He wouldn't pay me some of my wages, on account of my falling last Monday—you remember—Miss Sandra—I fell and some of th'eggs broke. He left me five shillings short."

Sandra was speechless. It had been the first time Sandra knew of that Old Sal had lost eggs. And this had not been her fault—Stevie had thrown a ball in her path. He was only three, and hardly to blame, though Sandra had given him a thorough scolding. Anybody would have tripped the way it had happened. The loss of six or seven eggs was not important; she and Joanie had helped Sal up and brought her into the kitchen for some strong, sweet tea, while the farm cats had come from all directions and lapped up the mess.

Sandra did not know what to do. She looked up at the house, to her father's window and the closed curtains there. It only took her a moment to decide.

"I'll speak to Mr. Craven," she said, and marched in the door of the office. He was alone there, standing at the table behind which were several shelves of thick old ledgers. He was locking the cash-box. He did not look pleased to see her.

"Ah, Miss Boone. What can I do for you?"

"Mr. Craven, why didn't you pay Sarah Burns her full wages?" she burst out. It seemed important to use Old Sal's

35

proper name. "It wasn't her fault she fell! It was my little brother's fault!"

He looked at her in some surprise, and she saw his mouth tighten into a straight line. He took the key and re-opened the cash box. When he spoke, it was in a rather embarrassed voice.

"Of course, of course! It was just a misunderstanding, Miss Boone! I thought—well, never mind—is she still here? I will certainly pay her her full wages. I'm so glad you cleared it up. I hope that you will forget this little misunderstanding?" he fixed her with his eyes. They looked very peculiar. He had pale eyes, and the black dot that everybody had in the middle of their eyes had shrunk to a tiny, tiny point. It unnerved her.

She ran out to get Sal, who came in and was paid her wages. Then Sandra went into the house, and to her room, running past several of the servants, who turned in surprised concern but did not say anything. She slammed the door and lay down flat on the bed. She needed to be alone for a few minutes. She had met something very unpleasant. She did not like Mr. Craven. A feeling of dread began to overcome her. Should she tell her father about this? She had the conviction that Mr. Craven would call it, again, a "misunderstanding" and that her father would accept it. She was sure of it. She got up and went to what was now her mother's room, to find her singing a lullaby to little John. She turned away and met Anna on the stairs.

"Our Sandra, you never play with me anymore!" Anna complained to her.

"And you never help me with the housework!" snapped Sandra.

Both girls burst into angry tears, bringing Mrs. Wall from the kitchen. She brought them there and gave them biscuits.

"Your father is getting stronger by the day, and you're blessed to have each other, for if I'd have had a sister, I never woulda fought with her, but I wasn't blessed with one, only four brothers. Now, Miss Sandra, you're to leave that pile of ironing until tomorrow, and go and run around the farm with Anna like you used. Everything will get done, don't worry. Miss Anna, maybe you'll help with putting away sheets and linens tomorrow after they're all ironed?"

"Why can't Joanie do more?" asked Anna crossly.

"Bless you, child, you don't understand nowt, do you? Joanie's not idle! She scrubs from mornin' till night. There's a lot of washin' and scrubbin' in a large family. She cleans out ashes and lights fires and does all the peeling of potatoes and vegetables and suchlike, and scours pots and pans and plates and all sorts after! Scrubs down kitchen—sweeps and turns out a room a day—next time you see Joanie, look at her 'ands. Near scrubbed to the bone, they are. Work doesn't get done by itself!"

Anna looked down, ashamed. Sandra had not realised either how much work Joanie did.

"Poor child," Mrs. Wall muttered after Sandra and Anna had run happily off. "Will Miss Boone's childhood ever come back to her? Father sick, Mother sufferin' on and off with her nerves, and that Mr. Craven—I don't know." She frowned to herself. Ben was sure that their new boss was very fond of opium, or maybe cocaine. He'd been to the Lodge and seen pipes and all the stuff. Everybody was afraid they'd put a foot wrong and be dismissed by him, but the Master and Mistress were very pleased with him.

CHAPTER NINE

Mr. Boone improved greatly in the summer months, but as the cold weather approached he relapsed. It always wore heavily upon him that his daughters had had no schooling of any kind. He taught them when he could. Their mother did not think they needed anything beyond reading and writing, except perhaps French. She had learned French from her governess so she began to give them lessons. She also decided to teach them sewing and regretted that the farmhouse had no piano, for she had learned.

Mrs. Wall was glad to see that as soon as John was weaned, Mrs. Boone began to take a greater interest in housekeeping. Perhaps someone had had a word with her about Sandra growing up too soon. Perhaps a neighbour after church on a Sunday, Mrs. Marsden perhaps, for it was murmured that Sandra Boone was an old head on young shoulders.

This was the year that Mr. Craven persuaded his employer to take the family away to Scarborough for the month of August. He had even mentioned it to Dr. Howard, who thought it a splendid idea. Sea air was healthy, and sea-bathing invigorating. The harvest was in able hands, and Dr. Howard urged them to go.

Mr. Boone got out an old map and spread it on the table, tracing the route from where they lived to the coast. "Are we going to take the train, Papa?" asked Stevie.

"No, Stevie, we'll take our carriage. But not to worry, lad, when we're in Scarborough, we'll go on day-trips on the train."

"Are you sure you want to drive there?" Mrs. Boone asked.

"I want to be upon the box again. And the children are old enough to take over from me if necessary, Harry is already quite the coachman. We'll break our journey in York, see the sights there, and stay the night at an Inn."

They set out full of excitement, were enchanted with York, and cheered at the first glimpse of the sea the following day as they neared the coast. To the children, Scarborough was like Heaven. Sun, endless sands, ice-cream, rocks to climb, kites to fly, donkeys to ride, and a castle to explore. They bathed every day, squealing at first with the cold, then becoming warm. Sandra had never had such a wonderful time in her life. And it was Mr. Craven who had thought of sending them to Scarborough! She'd almost forgotten that she once didn't like Mr. Craven. He was a wonderful help to Papa and all of them. The misunderstandings at the beginning had been ugly, but there had been no trouble since. Old Sal was still there, tending her flocks of hens and geese. She wrote to Aunt Maud, who was still in Russia, about it all. Maud did not write very often, but when she did, it was to describe her travels in her usual breathless style. She hunted wolves and bears and had no intention of returning to England.

The holiday did them all so much good, and the harvest was so ably looked after at home, that they went every year after that, and even brought the latest addition to the family when she was only three months old. Elizabeth Mary had been born the April before. They had other company as well— Mrs. Boone had written so enthusiastically of Scarborough to Mr. and Mrs. Knightley that they joined them, taking lodgings nearby. The couple were very popular with the children, as they spoiled them. The Knightleys came no more to Skipton, but holidayed with them in Scarborough.

The Boones also made friends with other families, some of whom came every August also, especially the Carmichaels, whose children were much the same ages as theirs.

The years went by, the farm thrived. They were doing so well that they erected new farm buildings and purchased efficient new machinery in the latest designs. Mr. Craven did it all. He modernised and improved everything. But it irked Mrs. Boone in particular that he kept his distance from them. He would not, for instance, ever pose with them for a photograph. She felt that he held himself superior to them in some way. The nursemaid, Betty, who had been with them some years now, said one day to her mistress that Mr. Craven had offered to invest money for the servants, promising a good return in ten years.

Mrs. Boone had mentioned it to her husband, who said he did not see anything amiss with it and was surprised that only two labourers, brothers Danny and Joe, had gone into the scheme.

Scarborough in August 1883 was blissful. Sandra was in her sixteenth year. She had grown into a tall, slim, pretty girl with clear skin, wide green eyes, and wavy hair, and noticed boys looking at her with admiration, which was embarrassing but rather pleased her too. Anna teased her about it, especially about the eldest Carmichael, Thomas. The families went on walks together, and Sandra and Tom were often walking side by side.

"Our Sandra's got an admirer," said her father to her mother one evening.

"Oh, she is far too young to think of marriage!"

"She is, that. But he likes her, I know he does. Carmichaels are a good old family, and Newcastle isn't that far away."

"Perhaps in a few years, she might think of him. But you'll miss her from the farm."

"I wouldn't stand in her way, Bella. Harry is nearly old enough now to help me with everything, and after he's finished with school, he'll work alongside me. By then, maybe Sandra will be married."

"We'll have two sons at school from September." Mrs. Boone sighed. Stevie was to join Harry at Hollyhill School for Boys shortly after they went home. "I will miss him."

Tom sought out Sandra for a walk the evening before the Carmichaels departed and asked her if she would be back the following year.

"Papa intends to bring us back every summer, it does us so much good, and our steward, Mr. Craven, sees to everything."

"I very much look forward to seeing you next year, Sandra."

Anna was a dreamer. She was sure that in time, both she and Sandra would meet rich young men who would sweep them off their feet and bring them to their mansions or castles, but now she saw Sandra becoming Mrs. Carmichael, and she was as pleased as if Thomas were a prince. The girls went for a long walk by themselves the following day, chatting and confiding and giggling about what they were sure awaited them in the future—they'd fall in love, get married and be happy. They went back to their lodgings and ate a hearty dinner with their family before going to sleep, as usual to the sound of waves splashing endlessly on the beach.

And so, to the only day of their holiday that they never liked —their last. They said goodbye to the seashore by taking a last walk and reminded themselves that they'd be back next summer. They piled into the carriage. Mr. Boone took the box, urged the horses on, and they were off.

They stopped at their Inn at York. By then, looking forward to getting home had taken over the sadness at leaving Scarborough. There was a piano at this Inn and they always had a sing-song around it. They set off in the early afternoon. Tired nearing journey's end, each had their own thoughts—Mr. Boone of the harvest, Mrs. Boone of getting the boys ready for school, Sandra wondering if Tom was in love with her and if she was with him, Anna dreaming of being bridesmaid to Sandra in the misty, distant future. Harry couldn't wait to see his dog, Shep, and take him for a good long run across the fields, and Stevie thought of his dog, Troy. John, on Sandra's lap, clutched his kite, asking if he could fly it at home, or did kites only fly in Scab'ro? Little Eliza slept on her mother's lap.

It was beginning to get dark early, and dusk was upon them as they approached their land. They lit the carriage lamps. They came at last to the big iron gate—and found it shut and padlocked.

"Good grief, what's this?" exclaimed Mr. Boone. He alighted the box. Mr. Craven's lodge was just beside the gate, and there was no light there. "Bad form, this is, the gate locked against us! Craven is out by the looks of things. We have to go around to side gate."

42

The side gate was locked by a bolt, but easily opened.

"It's too—too quiet, Papa!" called Sandra who was walking beside the carriage with Harry, to her father on the box as they took the winding path.

"Something's not right!" he replied, in a worried tone.

"No lights, not anywhere." Harry said. "And where's Shep? Come 'ere Shep!" he called out loudly.

They always gave the house staff leave when they were away, but they returned before the family, and had the house warmed and dinner ready. Now the old farmhouse loomed above them almost like a deserted ruin.

"I hope there hasn't been a fire." said her father tersely. "But the building looks all right. No fire, unless it was round the other side. Surely, they would have gotten word to us if that's what happened—" They were coming around towards the front door, and their suspicions that the house was empty became real. "Nobody here! Very alarming, this. Whoa."

He jumped off the box rather quickly and lost his breath for a moment. Sandra was staring at the front door. It was shut and had a bar nailed across it. *NO TRESPASSING* was boldly printed on a large notice.

Mrs. Boone alighted and joined them as they stared.

"What's the matter? Why are we barred from our own house? What can be the matter, Henry? The back door must be open."

Harry had slipped around in the darkness and came back to report that it was locked and had a bar across it also.

"This is unsupportable!" cried Mrs. Boone. "Has there been some misunderstanding about when we were to come back?"

Their father was pacing up and down the front, trying to see in through the windows in the dimming light.

"The rooms are bare." He said, turning around. "Come and see for yourselves. No furniture, nothing. All gone. There are just some things scattered on floors."

At this, Mrs. Boone became hysterical. "Robbery, murder and robbery, perhaps?" Anna flew to her side and tried to calm her.

They heard tired, old footsteps.

"Is that you, Squire Boone?" Old Sal's crackling voice was like a message from Heaven. She had come around the side of the house, carrying a flickering lamp, and clutching her shawl around her.

"Sal! Sal! Where—is everybody? What's—going on?" cried her father. Sandra barely took in the fact that he had become breathless.

"You don't know, sir? They came one day and took everything away, sir. Everything."

"Who? Who came, Sal?"

"Men, sir. Men with carts and wagons. They took everything out and away."

"But—but wasn't—Mrs. Wall here? Or Mr. Craven?"

"No, sir. They've all gone, sir."

This is a dream, thought Sandra.

"Where shall we spend the night? We have no food!" wailed Mrs. Boone. She continued to cry, repeating the questions over and over.

"Tell me everything—from the beginning, Sal." Mr. Boone leaned against the wall of the house.

"You don't know of it, sir? Mr. Craven said you would know of it. He went to tell you. It was the Friday after you left, sir. We went to get wages, for they was going on holidays, Mrs. Wall and Joanie and all, but not me; I don't like to go away. We went to offices and Mr. Craven said there was no money, sir."

"No money!"

"Yes, sir. No money to pay wages, sir. He said that there had been a—misun—misun—"

"Misunderstanding!" said Sandra immediately.

"Yes, Miss Sandra. With bank, sir. And he said he was going to Scarborough to fetch you down, sir. And he went, sir. Only you never came down."

"He did not come to Scarborough." Harry said.

"Where's Ben? Does he not come—to feed the stock?" her father gasped.

There awaited the greatest shock of all.

"Livestock is all gone too, sir. They drove them all away, sheep and cows and pigs, sir, and geese too and my little hens, nearly all of them, but our Margie hid, sir. And our Alexandra, she hid too. They're my cleverest." Her voice held admiration. Her listeners had hardly heard the end of her little speech. The livestock—their farm—was gone.

"This must be a bad dream," murmured Sandra to herself. "Yes, it must be. No, it's not. This, this is real. Papa!" She rushed to her father as he appeared to slump against the wall.

"Is there anything else you remember, Sal?" he asked with hoarseness, with great effort.

"Police were here too, sir. They put bar on door and said nobody was to—pass. Tes-pass." She pointed to the notice.

"Did you not say anything to anybody, Sal? Did you not ask them why?" Mrs. Boone screamed.

"I asked two men and they wouldn't say, ma'am. I ran back to my cottage, I was afeard they'd come and take my little things too, but they didn't, the man in charge, he was a toff, sir, with a top hat—he looked in and said, *nothing worth having here*, and off they went. Was I thankful!"

"Where is Craven?" Mr. Boone was mumbling. "Where is he? Why did he not get word—to me—Mrs. Boone, stop—that noise! Anna! Get your mother—smelling salts—"

"Anna, put Mamma into the carriage," Sandra said. "Papa, we'll go to the stables. There's nothing we can do now, it's nearly dark."

"I 'ave a bit o'bread and milk and a few eggs," offered Old Sal.

Sandra caught her father to support him, for he seemed to be about to collapse.

"To the stables, Papa. We'll shelter there for the night and find out more tomorrow."

"That's all we can do," he said, again with effort. Then he was silent as Sandra helped him into the carriage and took the reins to lead the team around to the stables. She glanced back at their house. Whatever the "misunderstanding" about all this, they would find out more at daylight. It would be all right, wouldn't it?

"Have you seen Shep?" asked Harry, rather desperately of Old Sal. He had been running about, calling his name, as Stevie had been, calling Troy.

"Oh, Master Harry, I—poor Shep!"

"Why? What's happened him?"

"He went for the toff, then he went for a policeman's ankles, and—policeman hit him with his stick, a 'ard blow. He yelped and run away. And Troy with him."

Harry burst into tears of anger. Sandra had to encourage and half-force him to unhitch the horses as their father had dropped down on a bale of hay, spent. Together they took the luggage from the top. Their mother was more quiet, but shivered and trembled. Anna exclaimed that her hands were icy-cold. Old Sal brought them bread and two hard-boiled eggs in a basket, and a jug of soured milk. Eliza and John were given the eggs, and the bread was divided among everybody. They passed the jug around, grimacing at the sourness of the milk. Finally, they fell asleep on the hay, the horses in their pens. At least they had water. Anna and Harry had taken one of the carriage lamps to go to the well and fetch water in a bucket.

"Mamma," Sandra heard Anna whisper. "Don't worry, Mamma. Jesus had to live in a stable too."

"You're my treasure, Anna." Her mother whispered back. "I will try to think on that. Yes, I will."

CHAPTER TEN

S andra got up at first light. Her father was motionless and looked grey in the dim light. She was deathly afraid. She bent over him and took his wrist to check his pulse. Dr. Howard had taught her to do that. He opened his eyes immediately.

"I'm a worry to you, Sandra."

"You should rest today, Papa. Your pulse is too fast."

"I will have to. My chest feels weak. But I'm breathing easier now." He closed his eyes again. "You have to go down to the lodge. Take Harry. If *he's* there, send him up. Why did he not let me know? He should have come immediately to Scarborough. He knew where we were." He sank back and shut his eyes again.

"Perhaps he met with an accident on the way there, Papa."

"Perhaps."

Harry was miserable about Shep and wanted to go and look for him.

"We have to go to lodge, and see if Craven is there," she said. "You can call Shep as we go, can't you?"

Together they ran down the drive, past the trees and shrubs lining it.

The lodge was empty and locked; a bar, too, across its front door. But they found a window open at the back. Harry wriggled in and unlocked the back entrance.

The kitchen was missing its table. They went to the bedroom. It was bare. The servant's room was bare also.

"Sandra, look, look here!" Harry had gone to the parlour, empty of furniture also. But there were some odd things thrown about, as if drawers had been emptied and the contents not worth seizing.

"It's Papa's name, everywhere—written over and over, on sheets of paper scattered on the floor—look—dozens of sheets!"

She picked up the sheets and scanned them, frowning.

"It's not just his name, Harry, it's his signature, or very like."

They stared at the papers, shaking their heads. Why would their father's signature be all over sheets of paper?

"It's as if somebody were practicing Papa's signature," Sandra said slowly. "Forgery. No, surely not. We shall have to take them to Papa. Is there anything else?"

There were a few discarded pipes, and sheets with notes and figures all over them; scatterings of a white powdery substance, but nothing else.

CHAPTER ELEVEN

Their father was awake. Silently, he took the sheets and pored over them. He could not speak, but constantly shuffled the sheets, as if not comprehending them, and stared into space.

Old Sal appeared with a fresh loaf of bread and two hard-boiled fresh eggs.

"It's the last of the flour," she said with sorrow. "If you can get flour, Miss Sandra, you can bake on my fire. And if you can get tea-leaves, I'll make tea for you."

"You are very kind, Sal." Sandra murmured. "Sal, have you any idea where Mrs. Wall and Ben and the others went—and why?"

"Miss Sandra, why they was not paid, were they? They had to find other places." Old Sal seemed bewildered as to why the question was asked. "Me, I had our Margie and Alexandra laying for me. And a bit of flour. And I could get no new place, could I? But I'm out of tea. If you was to go to town, Miss Sandra, maybe you'd get some tea."

"Of course—thank you, Sal."

That gave Sandra the idea of going to town. They'd need food for later on. Harry and Anna wanted to break into the house and retrieve whatever they found. Their father, overhearing as he examined the papers, looked up.

"Don't break in. You could be arrested and go to jail," he said sternly to Harry.

"But it's our house, Father!"

"I don't think it is, anymore."

"Oh, Henry, whatever do you mean?" cried Mrs. Boone. "Where shall we go? What shall we do? The boys have to be got ready to go back to school—"

"They won't be going, Mrs. Boone."

"No school!" Harry saw the bright side.

"I think that everything we possessed belongs to another entity, now."

"Everything?" exclaimed Sandra, horrified.

"Everything."

A few moments of horrified silence followed this. Her father threw the sheets of paper away from him and sank back on the bale of hay. His skin was a shade of grey.

"It's my fault. It's all my fault," he said. "What have I done? How could I have trusted him?"

Mrs. Boone began to cry hysterically. Sandra took the small children out of the stables and for a walk, while Anna went to her mother's side.

CHAPTER TWELVE

"**W**e have five pounds, and we must be careful how we spend it," cautioned Sandra to her sister and brother, who were to accompany her to Glendale village, or if necessary, to Skipton, to buy food.

"And don't tell anybody what's happened. Papa said so. He thinks there may be a way out of this, if Craven is caught."

"If he's caught, I want him to hang!" Harry cried. "This is my farm, my land, after Papa!"

"Don't say those things," Anna shivered. "Don't say '*after Papa.*' As for Craven, he did wrong, very wrong, but—Jesus loves him too."

Sandra did not feel so charitable but kept her feelings to herself.

Thankfully nobody asked them any questions, though Anna felt they were stared at, and they returned to the stables before dusk. Had twenty-four hours really gone by since last night? It seemed much longer. Old Sal boiled water for tea, and they had their first hot drink since York the day before.

"No bath!" said John with glee as they settled down for their second night on straw. "I love living in a stable!" He and Stevie had spent the day doing exactly as they pleased, outside and in, swinging from the wooden beams above down on top of the hay and sliding to the ground.

"Oh, you look like a ruffian," Sandra said fondly. "I've never seen such a grubby little boy in my life! Tomorrow, I'm getting a pail of water and I'm going to scrub you from head to toe."

"You haven't any soap!" was the gleeful reply.

"Mamma, what of our prayers?" Anna asked. "We should pray, for doesn't God still love us?"

"Henry?"

Sandra gave him his Bible. He opened it and read from the first Letter of St. Peter. Everybody listened, each with their own thoughts.

Faith is more precious than gold, Sandra thought. *We have no gold, but we still have faith. I pray it doesn't leave us!*

CHAPTER THIRTEEN

The family was very hungry again after two days, and Sandra, Anna, and Harry took the carriage as far as Skipton. Their father was breathless at the slightest exertion, their mother sitting motionless almost all day, numbed by the calamity that had befallen them. They had no money.

Their instructions from their father was to call on the Barracloughs for news of Mr. Craven. They turned in the gateway to the Georgian mansion just outside Skipton, and knocked on the door. Mrs. Barraclough received them. She did not know the whereabouts of Mr. Craven, but seemed uneasy, as if she had heard something, but wasn't sure exactly, and was afraid to hear more. Sandra burst out: "You know our farm, and house, have been seized—and we are in a desperate situation now—do you know anything about that?"

The woman looked genuinely horrified. "Seized! I did not know!"

They were shown out a few minutes later and proceeded to Skipton.

It must have been their empty stomachs, but Sandra and Anna had a dreadful quarrel.

"You're so worried about Papa," Anna had shot at her, "But what about Mamma?"

"Mamma is not like Papa! He takes all the responsibility, does all the worrying, plans, and tells us what to do. Mamma is just sitting on hay all day, without a suggestion occurring to her!"

"You favour Papa over Mamma, I know you do. Papa is bad-tempered. I know he doesn't feel well, but he shouts at us."

"Papa has all the responsibility, and I want to help him."

"Mamma does her best! She can't help it if she's nervous! But you can't forgive her for sending you out!"

"Whatever do you mean? Sending me out? Out where?"

Anna looked guilty and evaded her gaze. Eventually, she said:

"After you were born, Mamma sent you away to be looked after by a village woman. For nearly a year!"

Sandra was stunned. She felt as if an arrow had pierced her heart.

"How do you know?"

"Mamma told me."

"Of course!" Sandra's tone was bitter. "She tells you everything, doesn't she?"

"I shouldn't have told you, Sandra. It wasn't at all like what I said. Grandmamma Harvey told her to, and she was sorry after."

"It doesn't matter. Now I know why she favours you over me."

"I'm sorry for saying it, I really am."

"It's good to know where I stand." Sandra said with great bitterness.

There was a horrible silence between them as they reached the outskirts of Skipton, where they were to leave the carriage while they entered the town on foot.

"You know what we have to do here," Sandra said coldly.

"Yes, I do. We have no money, so we have to pawn Mamma's rings, and we have to beg."

"Then toss your hair and crumple your gown and look poor."

"How odd that we had to always dress up going to town before; now we have to look poor!"

They found the pawnshop and while they had no idea how to pawn anything, the owner seemed to know that, and took their mother's rings and gave them ten shillings. Anything else of value that Mamma owned was in the house—or had been.

"I don't know how much food this will buy," Sandra said. "And we have to pay the stable too, before we go home. How much is it to stable horses and a carriage for a few hours?"

"Buy us a bun, Sandie, I'm starving," Harry said. She bought three buns and they ate them sitting on a stone wall.

"Miss Boone! Miss Boone!" Sandra turned to see a familiar face coming toward her, clad in a shabby dress and shawl.

"Joanie! I'm so glad to see you!"

"Miss Boone, I'm so glad you're back. Why did your father not come from Scarborough to relieve us? I couldn't stay on. I had to find work! I don't like my new place; the mistress, she's bad-tempered. Mrs. Grant is her name. I want to come back to Glendale, and Mrs. Wall too. You do look poorly, Miss Boone. Are you all right?"

"We've had a great misfortune, Joanie. It seems until a misunderstanding is cleared up, we have no house, or farm. Or money."

Joanie's eyes became like saucers while she drank in this information.

"No 'ouse, nor farm, nor money! It wor' 'im!" she breathed. "It wor! Mr. Craven!"

Sandra said nothing.

"If the squire could see himself to payin' our wages that are due, we'd be very grateful," said Joanie then. "Mrs. Wall is lodgin' wiv 'er sister near Doncaster. I 'ave 'er address. Ben is workin' at Holly Farm other side o' Skipton. Danny and Joe're not goin' ter be 'appy with this news. They invested twenty pounds wiv Mr. Craven. Well 'es not likely ter come back, is 'e?"

"I will tell my father all you said," Sandra said. Joanie thanked her, made her goodbyes, and left.

Now, the moment they had been dreading had come.

"I'll stand on this corner here, you go and stand at the other end of the street." Sandra said.

"Why should I have to go to the other end of street? There's an alley up there! Stop bossing me, Sandra!" Anna shot at her. "You're always bossing me!"

"What's the matter with you girls?" said Harry crossly. "When I was driving, I could hear all kinds of shouting and crying from the carriage, I wish I had older brothers instead of sisters."

"You know you will have to beg too," said Sandra.

"We won't get anything. We don't look like urchins yet."

Sandra positioned herself at the place Anna did not want to take, and held out her hand to passers-by. Nobody seemed to see her. After a little while, Anna came running to her.

"Everybody is ignoring me," she wept, "I can't do this, Sandra, I can't! It's so humiliating! Don't make me, please! A horrible man told me I was in front of his—election bill or something —and told me to get away! He said the streets should be cleared of people like me!"

"We have to bring food home, and enough for a week." Sandra said roughly, resenting deeply that she had to be the tough one.

Harry joined them. He was rubbing a bruise under one eye.

"These fellows came up to me, all bigger'n me, and said they hadn't seen me before and I was to beat it. I argued and that's what happened."

"It's so horrible being poor!" wept Anna. "And it's all Papa's fault!"

"Is that the Misses Boone and Master Boone?" said a voice. Sandra looked up to see Reverend Marsden, looking at them with astonishment. "What can be the matter, children?"

Anna poured out everything in hysterical sobs. While she spoke, a little crowd gathered. Anna nudged Sandra after she had finished. *"Look, that's the horrible man."* She whispered.

There was a beefy middle-aged man, with a pompous air, staring at them.

The crowd was murmuring. The Boones of Glendale Farm were known and respected in the area.

"I must apologize, Miss." said the beefy man quietly to Anna with a bow. "I had no inkling of the circumstances." He straightened himself again, looked about him, tapped his cane on the ground and said, in a loud voice: "It is my opinion, Reverend Marsden, that this is a most deserving case and that it is our duty to help this family and alleviate their distress. Are you hungry, children? Please come, children, to my home. You will be welcome to refresh yourselves under my roof." He tucked his cane under one arm and began to walk away, looking over his shoulder to encourage them to follow. The children glanced at each other, looked for guidance from Reverend Marsden, who nodded his approval.

"When you go home, tell your father I will call on him." The Reverend said. "I will make enquiries in the meantime—surely somebody here knows what has happened, and that something should be done."

"Please bring Dr. Howard with you," Sandra had the presence of mind to say.

Mr. Grant led them to a large red-brick house on the edge of town by the railway station, and he greeted everybody on the way. He brought them ceremoniously around the back, and upon entering the kitchen sent the startled servant for his wife.

"Tell Mrs. Grant I wish to see her," he said.

Mrs. Grant. This is where Joanie works, thought Sandra.

They were bidden by the old Cook to sit at the kitchen table and were served some bread, cheese, and mugs of water. Mr. Grant came in and, before dismissing them, said that he would be "doing something for them." They thanked him and left. The food had been very welcome. All had saved some bread to bring home. Mrs. Grant did not appear.

The cook—Mrs. Grainger—gave them a sack of potatoes to take home, for which they were very grateful.

The girls were silent all the way home. Their true situation had just sunk in. They were poor and dependent; and that they had to have hopes of someone like Mr. Obadiah Grant —for they looked closely at the election bill when they passed—was truly enough to depress them.

CHAPTER FOURTEEN

Reverend Marsden kept his promise and visited, bringing Dr. Howard. The latter examined Mr. Boone and told him that though the shock had weakened his heart, it was likely to be a temporary situation and in resting as he had done, he had averted further damage. Dr. Howard saw Mrs. Boone as well. She was hardly speaking or eating. He told her husband that she was in deep shock. It should pass, but perhaps could become anger. He should be prepared, if so, to find blame heaped upon himself.

It would help her to busy herself with the children. The older girls were now taking care of them.

The gentlemen had already formulated a plan to help the family. Mr. Obadiah Grant had conferred with them and offered solid help. He was a man of property, owning several streets of cottages in Skipton. There one to become vacant in two days—he was offering it to the Boones, furnished, at low rent. But better still, he had tasked the gentlemen with offers of employment—Mr. Boone in his Textile Factory as Secretary, and one of the girls in his kitchen, as their own ungrateful kitchen maid had just given notice.

Mr. Boone had no choice but to accept all offers. He did not even know what his salary or wages would be. He knew of the Textile Factory—it was one of many that had sprung up in the area in the last forty years. There were many employees, mostly young women who worked long hours for very little wages.

And which of the girls would become a member of the Grant household?

"Not me," begged Anna. "I will housekeep and see to the children and Mamma."

"I suppose it will be me, then," Sandra said with bitterness.

"I have to get a job, Pa." said Harry bravely. "I can work on a farm with the horses."

"No! No!" Mrs. Boone spoke up, her voice loud and ringing. "You will not get a job, Harry, you will go to school! You are the only hope for your sisters and brothers! I intend to write to my relatives in Nottingham. And anything they can spare for us, is to be given to Harry's education."

Nobody dared to argue with her.

CHAPTER FIFTEEN

They moved the very next day to Primrose Lane, a narrow, crooked alley filled with small, ill-kept stone cottages. Their new home had three rooms and smelled of the drains from the communal latrine running behind the houses at the rear. Water would have to be obtained daily from the town pump, a ten-minute walk there and back, carrying two buckets. The floors were stone and there was no mat. A large, old-fashioned fireplace almost took up one wall. They would have to cook there. The bedrooms were dark and the bedsteads were rickety. The last tenant had left dirty, torn curtains. They could hear a child crying through the thin wall.

"We can't live here, Henry," said Mrs. Boone, horrified, covering her mouth and nose with her handkerchief. "We were better off in the stable."

"We were trespassing in the stable. We'll get used to it here, Bella. Until we have a bit saved, we'll abide here."

"What are we to do with the carriage and horses?" asked Harry. "Maybe Dr. Howard will let us keep them at his home."

"What's going to happen to Old Sal?" asked Sandra. "If Glendale is sold, she'll have to go to the workhouse."

The father did not have the answers.

A neighbour woman looked around the door.

"Would ye like a cup o'tea? I see ye don't have a fire yet. If ye'll come wiv me—"

She beckoned to Sandra and Anna, who, looking at each other in some puzzlement, followed her next door. They were heartened by what they saw there—a coal fire was lit and a kettle was singing. A man sat by the fire, smoking a pipe. A baby crawled around on a mat.

It was not impossible to live in a cottage.

"Welcome," he said, getting up to greet the girls. "We're the Sullivans. Got any coal yet, then? No? Tek a bit o'ours. Ye can pay me back when ye get some tomorrow." He shovelled several dozen lumps onto a piece of old newspaper.

"The neighbours are kind, Mamma." Anna said a little while later, as her mother looked doubtfully at the chipped cup in which the tea had come in. "Go on, drink it up."

Mr. Boone had one small shred of hope left that the situation could be retrieved. He had to visit the bank as he had as yet received no official explanation as to why his farm had been seized. Reverend Marsden had made enquiries—as they had suspected, massive loans had been taken out and the farm had become mortgaged. Where Craven was, and what his loans had been for, were a mystery to all.

Sandra went with her father to the bank manager. She sat in the old office surrounded by shelves of dusty ledgers, trying to understand how Mr. Firth had never had a suspicion about the many loans taken out by Mr. Craven, presenting documents supposedly signed by his employer. Mr. Firth was formal and distant with her father. She disliked him.

The signatures were good forgeries. Mr. Boone examined them with a heavy heart. There were loans supposedly for properties as far away as Scotland and even one for a tract of land adjoining his, land that had never been for sale. He recognised some documents that he had actually signed—signed at times when he had been very ill.

"There are still outstanding loans," said Mr. Firth. "Five hundred and sixty-seven pounds and sixpence halfpenny on a loan we provided for the construction of a 3-story house at Scarborough, where, I understand, you like to holiday."

"There is no such house." Mr. Boone said. "How did Craven persuade you to part with all that money in loans, when I never appeared in person?"

"It was well known that you were in poor health, Mr. Boone. I gave him the necessary papers to take to you, and they were returned to me, signed. I compared the signatures from older correspondence. They were the same."

Mr. Firth coughed. It was evident that he was not sure that the signatures were forged, or that Craven was guilty of fraud. In his mind, Mr. Boone had embarked on reckless sprees, buying properties and lands and equipment. Sandra thought that perhaps Mr. Firth would not admit that he had been taken in.

"I have nothing left," said Mr. Boone. Sandra's heart broke in two at her father's admission. How humiliated he must feel! She wished she could take it from him, all of it, and take it upon herself. The visit to the bank was a very unpleasant experience.

Mr. Firth acceded to Mr. Boone's request that they be allowed back into their house to retrieve the personal effects left there.

They paid a visit to the police afterward, to report the crime. But nobody had much hope of catching up with Mr. Craven. Instead of going to Scarborough as he said, he had probably left England by the nearest seaport.

Sandra, her father, and Harry went back to Glendale Farm and there, they sadly went through the rooms, picking up things from the floor, deciding if they should be kept or not. In the parlour, several of her mother's old letters were scattered about on the floor. Sandra bent and gathered them up. They might comfort her mother, or not, but they should not be left there. Halloa! A letter from Aunt Maud, addressed to her parents, and never opened! She would give it to her father on the way back to Skipton.

He opened it in the carriage, read it, and groaned deeply. He handed it to his daughter.

Dear Henry, Bella—I have just reached London and must write you a quick line before I go further on account of something important or it may be important or no, I do not know, but here it is: I was sitting in the train in Skipton just pulling out and I saw a man walking up the platform having just disembarked another train, I recognised him as a fellow known to the English in Paris—a criminal, had swindled people out of a lot of money—fortunes. I never met him, but he was pointed out to me on several occasions, his name was Alastair Johnson but that was not his real name and when I saw him at Skipton, I said to myself, I hope that is not Barraclough's cousin Alfred Craven who they are expecting at Glendale Farm! I knew I had to write just in case, to warn you.

How would you know him? He's average height, dark-haired, narrow face and thin and he has this odd movement with his mouth or his chin, a sort of twitch he got from opium or something. So Be Warned. In great haste and hope you are all well—you shall not hear from me for a long time until I am in Russia, Love Maud.

"Oh, Papa!"

"Your mother must have been given the letter, put it away intending to give it to me later. And forgot."

"Are you going to give it to her?"

"We will speak of it no more. What's done is done. We are both to blame. She, through forgetfulness, I through a foolish trust in my fellowman." He folded the letter and put it in his inside pocket.

They carried on.

"Papa, we are going to have to sell the carriage and horses, are we not?"

"Yes. I suppose so."

"Let's do it very soon, Papa, before the bank knows we still have them, and seizes them as well."

"And I know just who might buy them." said her father.

He knocked on the roof, causing Harry to halt, and gave him the order to turn in Barraclough's gate.

A mute Mr. Barraclough purchased them there and then, with cash. He spoke only to apologise profusely for his cousin. Mr. Boone assured him that he did not hold him responsible.

Harry was very unhappy at this, most recent loss. At least he'd found Shep, but not to keep. Both dogs had been taken in by a neighbouring farm. He was not allowed to take them home, because they could no longer feed them. Now he had lost his horses as well.

"I'm so thankful the bank didn't get the horses and carriage!" Sandra said. "Now we have money to keep us for a while, Papa!"

"We have to pay the servants," said her father bluntly. "They are due their wages. And we must do something for Old Sarah Burns. She was kind to us when we had nothing."

Sandra could not disagree. She turned her mind to her new situation. Tomorrow, she'd be working at Obadiah Grant's, reporting to his wife, Melinda Grant.

CHAPTER SIXTEEN

S he stood before her new mistress in the drawing room of their home. Mrs. Grant was dressed in a satin grey gown over-adorned with blue frills. She wore showy pieces of jewellery and enormous earrings. Her hair must have taken two hours for her maid to arrange, Sandra thought.

"You have been *somebody* up to now perhaps," said Mrs. Grant. "So, I feel I have to give you a special warning. Don't put on any airs here. You're a between-maid. You'll work in the kitchen and upstairs when needed. I want you to buy two black dresses, one to wash, one to wear. And four white aprons, one for the kitchen, one to be kept perfectly clean for serving upstairs, and two spare ones. You need two white caps. You will be outfitted at Clyne's Drapery and the cost will come out of your wages over three months—very fair, I think."

Sandra went downstairs wondering why she simply was not one or the other, a kitchen maid or a housemaid. There was a housemaid already, a cold, distant girl named June. Nobody at all made her feel welcome.

Mrs. Grainger, her boss in the kitchen, was not kind, again reminding her of "airs" as she put her to cleaning out a fowl. Over the next few days she seemed to take pleasure in assigning her the dirtiest jobs she could think of; a kind of revenge for her having had a life of plenty. Sandra did not argue. She did her work without complaint. She needed the money.

One day, Mrs. Grant had guests for afternoon tea.

"You're to serve when there be guests," said Mrs. Grainger grudgingly, while Rose cast her a resentful look. Sandra took care that everything was perfect on the tray, put on her clean apron and took the tea and biscuits up to the drawing room. A silence fell as she entered and set the tray upon the table to pour the tea to hand around to the four women gathered around the fireplace.

Why the silence? Why did she feel everybody's eyes upon her?

Then one of the guests spoke in a hushed tone.

"Is this—?"

"Yes," murmured her mistress. "One of the Boone girls. Their father is to begin employment next week with my husband."

Sandra flushed red but struggled to control herself.

"You are so noble, Mrs. Grant, so charitable, to help this misfortunate family. And your husband also!"

"It is our duty, Mrs. Harris. As one of the first families in Skipton, we have to set the example of charity toward the less fortunate."

Sandra's hands were trembling as she handed the tea around.

"That's all right, my dear," said Mrs. Grant when the cup shook a little. "You have been through a dreadful shock! You see, we are all your friends, are we not, ladies?"

The other women nodded and beamed in sympathy.

"Sandie will train as a domestic servant, and in time, I intend to ask her sister to join us too. At the moment, Annie is busy helping her mother in their *new house*." Mrs. Grant sipped her tea.

"Their new house?" chorused the women.

"Yes, one of the houses that we own happened to fall vacant, and of course Mr. Grant invited them to come to it."

"Such generosity of spirit!" said the third woman. "Without you, dear Mrs. Grant, this family would be in the—" she stopped, perhaps at last thinking of the housemaid's feelings.

"We know what you mean." said Mrs. Grant, nodding meaningfully. *"Thankfully* the workhouse has been averted." She looked up at Sandra with clear expectation of her expressing her gratitude. But Sandra was silent.

Mrs. Harris hinted: "Sandie, you must be very grateful, I am sure, to Mr. and Mrs. Grant?"

"Yes'm." Sandra grunted. She turned to get the plate of biscuits.

Mrs. Grant stormed to the kitchen a short time later.

"I demand of you," she angrily said, "To exhibit more politeness and fervour in serving my guests! Your manners were slovenly. If you do that again I shall dismiss you."

"You told me not to put on airs, Ma'am."

"Impertinent, ungrateful girl!" she flounced away.

To her surprise, Mrs. Grainger was laughing quietly to herself, and punched her playfully in the arm.

"You got gumption, girl! She 'ad it comin'!"

From then on, Mrs. Grainger was friendly. Sandra realised that she and the other servants were happy to see their mistress taken down a peg. They'd been afraid of Sandra in case she told tales upstairs, now they had no fears. The story spread, and she was very well liked as a result.

Sandra hoped that there would be an end of her having to serve upstairs as an exhibit of the Grants' … generosity, and she was right. She was never asked to take anything up there again. She worked in the kitchen early until late, slept in a tiny attic room, but the day she was paid was a relief. She went immediately to the cottage with her wages.

CHAPTER SEVENTEEN

Harry was sent to Nottingham to his mother's relatives, there to live with them and attend a day school. Sandra, on her day off, missed him from the family. Anna had almost turned into a drudge and had become bitter, blaming her father for everything, which he took stoically. Sandra felt it her duty to tell her Mamma's part in it also. Anna was aghast and had no intention of keeping silent—on Sandra's next visit, her mother drew her aside.

"I'm glad I know I was to blame as well," she said. "Now I cannot be angry with anybody except myself. Your father did the best he could. As I did, always, for you and the others."

Sandra thought of how she alone had been sent out to be fostered. It had smarted since she had heard of it. She felt her mother did not love her as much as she loved the others. But she held her tongue.

"You and Papa are weathering this together," she said instead.

"What other way is there?" she paused. "Are you very unhappy at the Grants, Sandra?"

"Not very."

"It was not the life we envisioned for you. We thought you would marry well."

"Mamma, it's not too late to give that hope up," Sandra said with humour. "Maybe an Earl passing through Skipton will see me from his carriage someday!"

She knew it would never happen, but it brought a rare, though sad, smile to her mother's face.

Mr. Boone was working now at the mill. He had a desk in a small, airless corner of his employer's office. He wrote letters and answered them. Mr. Grant did not ask very much of him; Mr. Boone was there to exhibit the Grant generosity to important visitors to the mill, who got the full sad history of the downfall of Glendale Farm in his hearing. He put his head down and pretended to be too busy to hear a word. He was paid very little—but was grateful on payday. With his health, no other employer would take a chance on him. The money from the sale of horses and carriage was gone.

It was a crushing day for everybody when they heard that Glendale Farm had been sold. But there was a silver lining to the cloud. The new owners were decent people, and knowing Old Sal had nowhere to go, kept her on. She came into town on a cart every so often, bearing fresh eggs, a luxury for them now. She had a full flock of hens—a Sandra, an Anna and an Elizabeth among them.

Mr. Grant put up the rent, Sandra found her wages withheld now and then for flimsy reasons. This put her family into great hardship from time to time.

One October day, Sandra was washing up after the breakfast at Grant House when she saw her father outside the kitchen door. He signalled that he needed to talk to her, so she went outside. He drew a letter from his pocket.

"This came a few days ago. It's from my cousin, Knightley. Read it." He paced up and down as she read the letter.

She read it and then looked at him squarely.

"No, Papa. No. Don't tell me you're thinking seriously of this."

"He will be brought up in a good house, as a gentleman. They will send him to school and to university. He will have a profession, the law perhaps, and will never be in want."

"Don't send Stevie or John away, Papa. If they want to help us, they can do so in another way."

"That is not their primary objective, Sandra. They want to adopt a child. A child of a blood relative. They've heard of our misfortune and think this would perhaps solve their problem and ease us."

"Have you asked Mamma?"

"She was very much against it, though she loves Emmeline Knightley. Then she was for it. Now she's against it again. And then, which child? Stevie or John? Harry will be all right, there's no need to consider Harry."

"What will my brother think, all his life, if you part with him? He'll think you and Mamma didn't love him enough to keep him."

"And yet, it would be out of love for him that we'd part with him."

Her father leaned on the doorpost. He seemed to have grown older in the last two months.

"Three children in Primrose Lane died last month." he said then, tucking the letter away in his pocket.

"Please let me know what you decide!" cried Sandra. She went about her work full of fear. Not even Mrs. Grainger's offer to teach her how to cook Chicken Dijon distracted her.

Where was God? What should they do? She prayed that night as never before, as she knew her father, mother, and Anna were praying also.

CHAPTER EIGHTEEN

John caught a fever, and for two days they feared for his life. That decided Mr. and Mrs. Boone to take up the Knightleys' offer to adopt one of their sons. It would be John, they thought, because he was younger and would be more able to adapt. But a fracas one day in the Lane changed their minds. Anna heard a commotion and looked out the door to see a company of boys, Stevie among them, running into the Lane as if fleeing. Stevie ducked in the open door. He took a fresh bun from his pocket, broke it, gave some to John who wolfed it down.

Stevie admitted to his father that evening that he had become friends with a gang of lads who stole. They were hungry, so they stole food. He promised not to do it again. But within a week, the same thing happened; only this time a policeman brought him home and issued a stern warning that next time, he would be arrested and sent away.

They began to see that for Stevie, a change of circumstances was essential. Suddenly the offer of adoption, painful though it was, seemed like a gift from God.

Mr. Boone took him for a walk the following Sunday after church. When he got tired, they sat on a wall, and there he explained everything to him. At nine years old, Stevie barely understood adoption. He was made to understand that his parents were not punishing him. He had one important question—would the Knightleys give him all he wanted to eat? He was hungry all the time now. When his mother saw his bright, hopeful eyes upon their return, she knew that the decision was right. She went to him and embraced him in tears, rumpling his fair hair.

Mr. Knightley came himself to collect him in November. He brought a letter from his wife to Mrs. Boone, which was a great comfort to her in its warmth and promises to love her little boy as much as she did, if that was possible. The entire family went to the railway station. Sandra thought her mother was very brave, but her eyes told the real story— there was utter heartbreak there, and in her father's also. Mr. Knightley knew that this was no occasion to display his own joy. Everybody knew that loneliness would envelop Stevie later on, perhaps when he lay in bed in a strange room, or had nobody to play with, or at Christmas-time. They would write to him of course, to Master Knightley, the name by which he would be known from now on.

Sandra went straight back to work, parting from her family at the station gate. Her mother was already in a fit of weeping, and Anna was supporting her as they walked slowly along back to the Lane. Eliza held one of her father's hands and John the other—very tightly—was he afraid he would have to leave as well? Sandra watched them go, and her heart broke in sorrow for all of them. She walked back to Grant House with a sad, heavy feeling oppressing her chest.

"I 'ope nobody saw you," said Mrs. Grainger. She had not sought permission from Mrs. Grant, but Mrs. Grainger had told her she would look the other way if she wanted to run to the station to see her brother off.

At least, Mrs. Grainger was on her side now, and was determined that when she retired, in a year's time, that Sandra would take her place. And so it happened, for Mrs. Grant saw that she could have excellent cuisine, very cheaply indeed, in Sandra Boone.

CHAPTER NINETEEN

1888

Even though Mrs. Grant knew she had a fine cook, she never allowed Sandra to know this. One day she came down to berate her after her lunch guests had left.

"The chicken was overdone," she barked.

"It's very hot weather, Ma'am. I was afraid it had gone off a bit—so I gave it a little extra—just made sure there wasn't any pink."

"It was not 'gone off a bit' as you put it. I sniffed it myself this morning."

Sandra made no reply. The chicken had spoiled a little. She thought of the trouble she'd have been in, if her guests had become sick from it!

"Oh, and I am cancelling your day off tomorrow. Mr. Grant has important guests to dinner."

Sandra had not had a day off for two weeks now. Every day there was someone important coming to lunch or dinner.

"I'm sorry, Madam. I promised my sister I would sit with my mother while she goes to the doctor. She has headaches this long time past."

"Headaches! Everybody has headaches! But we just put up with it instead of running to the doctor. Isn't your younger sister old enough to stay with your mother? What is the matter with your mother, Sandra?"

It was a cruel question and Sandra did not answer. Everybody knew that Mrs. Boone suffered from her nerves and was apt to spend days sitting in a corner, silent. Sometimes it was difficult to get her out of bed. Eliza was too young to stay with Mamma. Anna's headaches were getting worse and she had never seen a doctor. But these details were none of Mrs. Grant's business.

"And is your father in good spirits these days?"

Another cruel question, designed to remind her that her father was dependent on the Grants.

"He is keeping well."

"Good. Now as to tomorrow, you may leave for a few hours in the morning, and we will manage luncheon on our own. But be back by two o'clock."

"Yes, Madam. Madam—my wages—?"

"We'll see to it on Friday. Oh, by the way, I haven't seen you wear the hat I gave you last month. Is it not to your liking?"

"It is a good hat, Mrs. Grant." Sandra felt the humiliation. She could never afford a new hat and had to make do with her employer's cast-offs. She also wore a dull grey jacket that had been hers.

Mrs. Grant left the kitchen with an arrogant swish of satins. Sandra sat down and put her hands over her face. *We'll see to it on Friday* meant that Mrs. Grant would make her mind up on Friday. If she was not pleased with tomorrow night's cuisine, her wages would be withheld again. But Mrs. Grant was impossible to please.

Again, she pondered leaving. She did this every day. But the conclusion was the same—if she left, there could be retaliation. It seemed so hopeless, and yet, there was always hope. She always found a little hope in her despair, for without it, she knew she could not go on.

She walked to Primrose Lane the following morning.

"Oh dear, another hat," Anna said when she saw her. "A muddy colour, rather horrible, I think. She stripped it of everything nice before she gave it to you, didn't she?"

"It's ugly enough, but I shall trim it with yellow ribbon." Sandra tossed the hat on the back of a chair.

"Will we ever be able to afford a new hat again?" Anna asked with longing. She was turning eighteen soon, but she looked thin, worn and harried. She made a fresh pot of tea from the breakfast tea leaves and they sat at the table.

"Mamma," she called into the inner room. "Sandra's here." Sandra realised her mother wasn't coming out to see her, so she went to the room. Her mother was lying in bed, staring at the ceiling. Sandra bent and kissed her.

"Hallo, Mother."

"Sandra." Mrs. Boone's eyes did not even leave the ceiling and Sandra sighed. "Do you want tea Mamma? Will you not get up, and come out and drink it?"

"No, no tea. Go out and drink yours."

Sandra did as she was bidden.

"You have to get out of Grant's," Anna said to Sandra. "Don't be afraid that they'll let Papa go as revenge; poor Papa is an exhibit of Grant generosity, to be displayed whenever there are visitors, or so they can say that they are still supporting the unfortunate Boones from Glendale. Ugh! How they anger me!"

"Anna, your headaches come on always when you get angry, so don't get angry. Where are John and Eliza?"

"John is hostlering in the town. He gets a few pennies from it. And Eliza is playing with her little friend down street."

The air in the cottage was insufferable in summertime, but even so, the tea tasted refreshing. Sandra had baked several pastries extra the day before and hidden them so that she could take them home. Anna's face lit up.

"Will we ever get used to poverty?" she asked.

"No, I don't believe we will. Has there been any letter from Harry or Stevie?" she asked, to change the subject.

"Oh, Stevie wrote! He's better than Harry for writing, because Mrs. Knightley makes him, probably! He's enjoying his summer holidays, and they are off to France and Switzerland for July and August. But here—read it yourself."

Sandra smiled as she read the letter. Again it gave her hope that better times must be in store for all of them. Harry, still in Nottingham, had been apprenticed to a legal office. He studied very hard, was passionate about the law, probably because of what had happened to his family. He had returned to them once for a visit and had not really enjoyed it, Sandra thought. He had forgotten how horrid the cottage had been and how listless and sad his mother was, after the euphoria of seeing him had worn off. It angered him deeply to see how unimportant his father was in the office where he worked and how Mr. Grant spoke to him. He had gone gladly back to Nottingham.

"He wants to get the farm back one day," Anna said sadly. "I don't think he has a hope."

"But we all have to have something to work towards, Anna."

"I have nothing."

"You should have, Anna."

"No, I'm stuck here," Anna whispered. "She needs me. But everything she suffers, I suffer, Sandra. As if it were me who was suffering from this dreadful *melancholia,* the doctor calls it."

"And that's the cause of your headaches?"

"Possibly."

"You used to have dreams. Isn't there any young man around here whom you like?"

"Oh, not around here," Anna bit into a pastry. "I wouldn't marry into these hovels for a fortune. No, no hope for me. But there is hope for you—do you have any dreams, Sandra?"

Sandra smiled a little. She indulged sometimes in dreams, particularly when Mrs. Grant had scolded her unjustly.

"I want to see London," she said, putting on a loud, posh accent. "I want to throw that old brown hat in the Thames, and I want to buy a new scarlet one with peacocks feathers. I want to be a lady in Mayfair, and to be taken in a fine carriage to the Savoy Theatre to see a Gilbert & Sullivan opera."

"Taken by whom, my Lady?" asked Anna mirthfully.

"By nothing less than a Duke, of course," Sandra said airily.

They both burst into laughter. Then Sandra became serious again.

"But I know I'm going to have to leave Grant House soon. And not just because of Mrs. Grant either. There's her husband."

"What of him? I didn't know that you ever saw him."

"He comes down to kitchen sometimes, always when Madam is out, or gone to bed. It makes me feel very uneasy, I can tell you."

"What does he say?"

"He walks about and talks about horses and business deals he made. As if I cared! If he tries anything, I'm running out of Grant House and never going back. I keep everything packed in my carpet-bag and have it ready in the pantry, hidden. Even my money, what little of it I have. I keep it around my neck, always."

"Be very careful, Sandra. I'm going to worry about you. But you should walk out if he tries any funny business. If he evicts us out of revenge, I will tell Papa everything. But I doubt he will, because then we might start some talk. He'll want to play it down. His reputation is everything to him."

"Anna, look at the time! You had better go to the doctor, because I only have a few hours."

"My headache's gone. Having the cuppa with you did it, and the laugh. But I will take a turn down by Eller Beck where the air is fresh."

"I suppose no word from Aunt Maud?"

"Oh no, maybe she's been eaten by a Russian bear. Poor bear! Sandra, if you have to leave Grant House in a great hurry— where will you go?"

"I will come here before I decide anything."

She went in to kiss her mother goodbye before she left. Her heart was torn between pity and censure for the woman. On the one hand, it must be hellish to feel every day was so dreadful a burden that you could not even get out of bed. On the other, why could her mother not make the effort?

"I heard you say you might go to London," her mother said, searching her face.

"I don't know, Mamma." Oh dear, what else had her mother heard?

"It might be good for you to go there. The Grants are horrid people. Go soon, if you go. And Sandra—I might not see you again."

"Oh Mamma, I will come back to visit—before I leave, and then, as often as I can."

"Sandra, just in case. I want to tell you something. You think I love Anna more than you. That's not true. But what is true that you were sent out to be fostered, and I wasn't strong enough at the time to object—after a long labour—I was very tired, and my mother persuaded me. I tried to get you back, but the weather was bad and we could not go out and fetch you—" Tears started to her mother's eyes.

Sandra was distressed now at her mother's distress.

"It doesn't matter, Mamma!"

"Are you sure, dear?"

"I'm sure, Mamma!"

"I always regretted it. And your father was furious."

"Was he?" Sandra had not heard that detail.

"Yes, not with me, though, but with my mother. Goodbye Sandra." Her mother took her head between her hands and kissed it.

"Goodbye, Mamma."

"Sandra, that is a dreadful hat."

"I know, Mamma."

"Why do you wear it, then?"

"I can't afford another, Mamma. You know the way it is!"

"Oh, yes." Her mother dropped her hands to the sheet and seemed to sink further into the bed. Her gaze returned to the ceiling once again as an emptiness came over her eyes. Sandra watched her with a growing sense of despair.

"Goodbye, Mamma."

There was no reply. Her mother was somewhere else.

Sandra left the cottage with the familiar feeling of dejected helplessness.

CHAPTER TWENTY

Her father was outside the kitchen door again, and she went out to see him.

"Anna told me about your concerns here," he said flatly. "I want you to leave this house, and get another situation, anywhere. I will not have my daughter compromised!"

"Don't worry, Papa. I'm old enough to look after myself."

"I know what he's like, Sandra. The poor girls in the mill—so promise me, daughter."

"I promise, Papa! I didn't mean to worry you, by telling Anna! She tells everybody everything!"

Her father smiled.

"I don't know how we'd have got through the last four years without my two eldest daughters," he said, putting an arm about her shoulders. "You've held the family together, you and Anna, young as you were. Harry did his share too. Sandra, you might find yourself in need of this."

"Papa!" It was two guineas. She tried to give him back one. He refused.

"I saved them. You have my blessing, Sandra. You've always been a blessing to me, and always will be. Look after yourself."

"Oh Papa, if I leave Skipton, I will go to Primrose Lane of course, to say goodbye!"

"If you have to make a quick escape, make for the railway station. Don't underestimate his power to hurt you. If he finds you in Skipton, he may take revenge, he accused poor Hetty Barton—in the mill—of stealing. She spent three nights in jail before the skeins *turned up.*"

He embraced her and turned away, trying to hide his tears. She watched him out the back gate that led to the mews.

The summer went on without incident, and Sandra was beginning to feel that there was no danger to herself. One day in early August, Mrs. Grant dressed up and went out for the afternoon for her monthly meeting of the Skipton Women's Charitable Trust. She and three other women interviewed destitute women who were asking for charity. They had to judge whether they were deserving of charity or not and if so, they gave them something. If not, they were sent upon their way.

The housemaid had the afternoon off and the manservant came to the kitchen to say that he was going out to do several errands for Mr. Grant, who was staying in. The governess had taken the children to the Park. Sandra did not like that it was only Mr. Grant and herself in the house. At four o'clock, she had to take the tea up to him.

He was in his study, but not behind his desk.

"Put the tray down there, Sandra." He indicated the table. She did so and as she turned around, realised that he was standing with his back to the door, staring at her and smiling.

Her blood ran cold.

"Sandra," he began, "You have surely noticed that I have been paying a lot of attention to you."

"You are a married man, sir!"

"Yes, that's true, but I am not a satisfied man, Sandra."

"I will hear no more. I beg you to allow me to pass," she pleaded. She was not far from the window, and flicking her eyes desperately in its direction as a possible, but hopeless means of escape, a sudden thought occurred to her.

"Miss Aynsley is crossing the street with the children," she said quickly.

He frowned and moved toward the window to see for himself, and she picked up the tray and threw it toward him while she fled out the door—thank God he had not locked it! —and ran as fast as she could down the back stairs, through the back hall and out the back door, pausing only to take her packed bag from the pantry. As she ran, she threw off her apron and cap, and passing the nail beside the door, crammed her hat on her head and grabbed her grey jacket from it, pausing briefly to pull it on to disguise her uniform. She ran through the mews, the end of which was very near the railway station. She turned toward it.

Suddenly she was on the platform, breathless. There was a train standing there, its engine puffing steam, a guard coming up the side closing the doors ... slam ... slam ... slam ...

"Wait," she cried, running toward the door he was about to close. "Wait for me!"

"Come on, Miss! Hurry up! We're late!" the guard snapped impatiently, and half-lifted, half-pushed her up into the train, slamming the door behind her as soon as her feet touched the floor.

"All clear!"

The train jerked forward, almost causing her to lose her balance. It began to chug slowly out of the station. Sandra, not even seated yet, caught a glimpse of Mr. Grant running onto the platform. He was looking frantically around, his face the picture of rage, shouting something to the guard. Then he was gone from her sight.

A young lad jumped up and obligingly put her bag up on the luggage rack, and a woman made room for her in a seat, smiling and remarking that she had better catch her breath. Sandra thanked her and sat down, recovering a little. Her heart was racing, pounding in her chest. Her head had to catch up with the events of the last ten minutes, for it was hardly more than that. Was she really leaving her situation, her family, Skipton? She felt unbearably hot, but did not take off her jacket, as she would look very odd travelling in servant's garb. Wild thoughts occurred to her—Mr. Grant might go to the police and accuse her of stealing and she'd be followed and arrested. He must have come out his front door and glimpsed her as she came out of the mews and sped toward the station. But she could not be arrested when she only had her own belongings with her. She began to relax a little.

Where would she be tonight? Where would she sleep? When the guard came around to check the tickets, she still did not know where the train was going as he made his way down the carriage.

"Leeds?" he asked the woman next to her.

"Yes," said the passenger.

"Leeds, please," she said as smoothly and confidently as she could, as if she travelled this way every week.

"Return?" he waited for an answer. "Miss, return? Or one-way?" he sounded a little impatient.

"I'm not coming back," she heard herself say.

CHAPTER TWENTY-ONE

S he tried to look as if she had been in Leeds many times, and walked with confidence out of the station. She found a Railway Hotel nearby and booked a room, feeling that the clerk disapproved of her being alone. She ate a good breakfast as it was included in the two shillings and sixpence.

She made her way to the station early. She wondered if anybody from her family knew that she was already gone, but she did not want to contact them from Leeds.

There was nothing for her in Leeds, and she was going to London. Wasn't there something for everybody in England's capital, and isn't that why it was bursting with life and new residents and growing year by year? She would make her way there, and make her life.

There was one other good reason to go to London. She understood that Hove was not far away, and she could be near Stevie. She could stay with the Knightleys until she found her feet. She would be welcome there.

She was a few hours aboard the London train when she remembered that the Knightleys were spending the rest of the summer abroad. She tried to calm herself, but her thoughts were a jumble inside her head, and every mile south only increased her panic.

What was she going to do in London? As the train sped south, she had plenty of time to think, and was relieved that she had boarded an early train. She would arrive in daylight.

Her heart beat a little faster as the train passed towns and villages with more frequency, and finally it seemed that they were in a maze of railway tracks—they were in a city—a large and busy place as it slowed and entered a cloud of hissing steam. They had reached Euston Station.

Disembarking, she found herself in an enormous, thronged hall with ceilings as high as a cathedral, and she looked up and around with wonder. Following her fellow-passengers, she passed through a magnificent archway and onto a handsome square with fine buildings on either side of her. *London! She was in London!* Her heart beat with excitement.

She would have to find work in the next day or two, for shelter as much as to earn money. But first, she had to let her family know where she was. She'd have to send a telegraph. Where could she telegraph from? She'd never sent one before!

She espied a hotel and walked toward it. The porter looked her up and down—she was shabby, she knew. She waited behind a group of men queueing at the desk. The women were seated in the foyer. When it was her turn, she made her request to the clerk. With the paper in front of her, she was not sure how to use it—and asked the clerk, but he was busy.

"I can help you, Miss!" the boy offering help was well-dressed, and perhaps waiting for his father who was in the queue. He was about nine or so, the age when they love to impart information. "Write your message there. It has to be very short. They tap it out in Morse Code!" he said.

"Why, thank you, you are kind."

"Miss, do you know, that soon people will be able to talk to each other through telegraph lines? I can't wait for that!"

"Edward!" his mother whispered loudly from a seat nearby.

"My uncle has spoken through the telegraph!"

"Edward, come over here, and stop bothering people!" said his mother again.

"He has been a help to me," Sandra smiled, defending the boy who reminded her of Stevie who had been about the same age when he had been adopted by the Knightleys. The woman smiled back but told her son to sit down and not to wander around everywhere he wanted.

"But I want to go up on *that*, Mamma. Say I can, please …!"

That appeared to be the little cubby hole in the wall that people were stepping into, and the door shut and then a few minutes later it opened again, and a completely different set of people got out! It carried people to the upper floors and down again. She had heard of elevators but had never seen one before. London was astonishing!

Having sent her telegraph to Skipton Post Office, Sandra realised she was very hungry. It would not do to eat at a hotel though; her money was dwindling fast. She began to walk with a dual purpose, that of finding a place to sleep and to eat. Everywhere she went, she was fascinated by the tall buildings, the liveried equipages, and the elegantly dressed people. It seemed everybody in London was doing very well indeed! She'd write to Skipton as soon as she could and tell them all to come directly.

But she had no references for a job, and that began to occupy her. No family would take a person into their home without references as to character as well as skills. Even all the places to eat were beyond her budget. At one hotel, a porter, no doubt seeing she was new to the city, and hot and tired, hurried after her, and told her that if she walked toward the Thames, or got a train to a place called Whitechapel, where he was from, that she'd find accommodation more to suit her budget, and in the meantime, if she was hungry, and she looked as if she was, he knew a reasonable place not far away. He pointed her in the right direction and she, going down a side street, found a café that provided her with a good meal of soup, bread, and meat for a shilling. At last, she felt refreshed and ready to resume her quest. She walked towards the Thames, following his directions, and soon realised she was part of a crowd of people who were crossing over a bridge by cart, carriage, or on foot. *Was this London Bridge?* Her pulse quickened. She was in a throng of tradesmen, costermongers, flower sellers, carts, and carriages. She slowed her pace to marvel. From where she was, she saw another bridge, shaped like the letter H. Was that Tower Bridge? Her mind raced to the Tower of London, and she imagined the two Princes who had perished there, and Queens Anne and Katherine. Her father used to read to them about the Kings and Queens of England.

"Miss! Move along there!" she'd stopped, causing a man carrying a heavy sack of tools on his back, to halt suddenly.

"Oh, I beg your pardon!" she said, thinking that in London, people moved faster, and she had to keep pace. But where was she now? Was she near Whitechapel? She asked a policeman—no, it was the other side of the river whence she came.

She recrossed the bridge, this time looking out past the other bank, and then found a cheap boarding house close by. The landlady was a down-to-earth chatty woman who, upon hearing she was new in the city, warned her to be on her guard.

"Whitechapel's not safe these days," she said darkly. "We 'ad a murder 'ere only yesterday. Poor defenseless woman, no better than she should be, mind you, but I'm not a person to judge, I leave that to my Maker. They're to be pitied, those unfortunates. Stabbed this one was, by a maniac."

"I won't be out after dark," Sandra said.

"But be careful anytime. Mind you don't get robbed neither."

But Sandra was too enchanted with London to be greatly concerned. Her mind was full of the astonishments of England's capital city. But she was tired. Had it been only yesterday that she fled Skipton? Yorkshire seemed so far, far away! Another world!

She fell asleep with the sounds of the city in her ears—was it ever quiet? Blasts from ships' horns woke her. Dogs barked on and off. The clop-clop of horses, the scrapes of carts, and the cries from milkmaids and fruit sellers reached her as light shone in through the thin curtains. She jumped out of bed and looked eagerly out the window. London was moving already! And she had no time to lose. London was very exciting, but everything was very expensive and she would have to find work today, if not as a cook, as something less!

CHAPTER TWENTY-TWO

M r. Clement Lark walked down High Street at Whitechapel in his usual reflective mood. He turned onto Castle Street and from there, took a right turn which brought him into Cobham. This street had been graceful in Tudor times, and the house of a prominent citizen then, a Mr. Oakes. It had been a splendid dwelling in its day and was still Cobham Street's tallest building. Even as the city moved out to enclose Whitechapel, and the other homes and businesses in Cobham Street were torn down, the Oakes House stayed. It was lofty and untouched, towering above the newer buildings.

Four generations had passed since the Oakes House—or just The Oakes as it was now known—had been purchased by a Mr. Laurence Lark, and the house turned into a club. Gentlemen met here to read the newspapers, play chess, debate, and dine. Drunkenness was frowned upon and debauchery forbidden. Laurence's son Clement carried it on. But his heir, Albert, neglected it. The club deteriorated, staff left, and Albert died in 1887, leaving it to his nephew, a man of twenty-six from Chelsea named Clement Lark.

He stopped and looked at the house and wondered for the umpteenth time if he could restore it to its former success. It was still a sound structure; he'd put on a new roof, modernised the kitchen and made essential repairs. It had a fresh coat of paint. From the outside, it looked very well, its distinctive Tudor design a contrast to everything around it. He had added the small porch inside the front door to keep the draughts at bay.

The porch opened into the large tiled hall. There was a fireplace at the far end and an old piano beside it. Small tables ran along the side walls for dining, and larger tables in the middle for reading and other leisurely activities. He had put in a billiard table. An oak staircase led to the rooms above. But overall, the interior was old and shabby, and the floor tiles chipped. It was dark, and even in daylight hours the gaslights flickered.

His two employees instantly began to look busy. One took a broom and began to sweep; the other flicked a duster over a bookcase. Clement sighed.

The man with the duster, a handsome, debonair type who could play the piano and occasionally entertained the guests, approached him. "Mr. Lark, I need to have a word, sir. I'd like to give notice. I've obtained another position."

"That's good news, Davis. Where is it?"

"*The Canterbury*, sir. In Lambeth."

There was a snigger from the other worker, a man named Whistler. Davis looked annoyed.

"That's quite a step up for you then, Davis." Clement was surprised. The music hall was well-known.

"He's got a sweet'eart there, sir, a soprano." Whistler put in.

"I say! Well done, Davis!"

"She's Miss Gibson. A solo artist."

"That's true, Mr. Lark," Whistler said. "I met 'er an' all."

"Congratulations, Davis. When do you start?"

"Er—tonight, sir."

"Tonight. That isn't notice, Davis. But I'm not a man to stand in the way of opportunity, or romance. I'll pay your week's wages and you're free to go."

"Thank you, sir! That's good of you, not to make a song and dance, no pun intended."

"I'd like you to do one thing for me, Davis. Talk us up. *'The Oakes, where I used to work, has the finest food and drink in the East End and it stays open until one o'clock in the morning.'* Promote us."

"I'll be glad to, sir. Even the fib about the food."

"I say, that's low, that is," said Whistler, who was acting cook since the last one had left. "I do my best! Fact is, I never learned, and I think I've done an excellent job with the pie 'n mash."

"That's the only item on the menu," smirked Davis.

"The blokes who come in 'ere, that's all they look for, innit."

"I'm searching for a cook, Whistler," said Mr. Lark. "But it's not that easy to find a man who can do eel pie for one man and something—*French* perhaps—for another. It seems to be either one or the other."

"Guv'nor, I'll never cook snails, never. I mean, that's not civilised, to eat snails."

"Snails will never be on the menu. Maybe some *coque au vin* for variety, but no snails."

"coke o'wha'? The only coke I know is the kind of coke you burn from coal."

"The dish King Louis the Fourth wanted every Frenchman to be able to afford on Sundays. Or perhaps that was *poule au pot*. 'Chicken in the pot.'"

"And you're supposed to char the chicken with coke, is it?"

"Forget I said anything, Whistler, it's all right. Bring me a cup of tea, will you? And can you make sure the water is at a rolling boil this time?" Mr. Lark sat at his usual table, the one near the staircase, where his post awaited him. Bills, bills, and more bills. Would he ever be able to make this club run well again?

"Oh Guv'nor, I forgot to tell you. Your mother's 'ere. She's restin' upstairs."

Clement nodded, but inwardly sighed. He knew why his mother was here.

CHAPTER TWENTY-THREE

Sandra thought it wisest to stay a second night in the boarding house, so she was able to leave her belongings there while she went out to look for work, and explore at the same time. To her dismay, this area of London showed her that not everybody did well here, and perhaps she should not summon her family yet. The deeper she got into Whitechapel, the more sights she met that reminded her of Primrose Lane and others like it at Skipton. Narrow streets, decrepit houses, broken windows. Filthy refuse and stinking drains. Badly nourished, barefoot urchins, and many, many more of them than Skipton. Some streets had a crowded, needy, desperate, hungry feel. Women in rags standing about, as if waiting for something. Unkempt men lounging in doorways, staring at her. She felt bitterly disappointed, but scolded herself for her naiveté. It was too good to be true, wasn't it, she said to herself ruefully, that London streets were paved with gold.

Had she made a mistake coming here?

She didn't want to work in Whitechapel—she turned around and, getting her bearings by now, walked to the better areas of the city she had seen yesterday. Throughout the morning, she knocked on doors and was turned away. Twice, she was brought in and presented to the housekeeper. And upon each occasion, upon hearing that she had no references, she was turned out. Worry began to gnaw.

Without references, finding a situation would be almost impossible, it seemed. Why had she not thought of this?

A summer shower poured down, and she turned her steps back to Whitechapel. She had enough money until tomorrow, so she'd go back to her lodgings and ask for pen and paper to write to Reverend Marsden for a character reference.

As she walked along, she thought she was being followed by a rough sort of man, perhaps one of those who had stared at her from a doorway, and remembered the landlady's sober warnings. Or was her imagination playing tricks? She did not want to panic, but she had to be prudent. She stayed calm. She turned a corner and, thinking he would catch up with her any minute, she pushed in the door of the first house. She was in a porch with a tall plant stand, which she tried to hide behind. To her relief, she saw him pass by. She decided to wait a little while before leaving this place though.

She turned and peered inside the window on the inner doors and realised it was a public place, a restaurant, with tables along the sides and a staircase going up. The place appeared to be empty, but then she saw a man sitting at a table. His manner interested her—he had a pile of letters in front of him and was holding his head in his hands.

Still peering, she saw an old woman in a purple gown and white lace cap come downstairs. With a frown, she began to speak to the man. His mother, perhaps? She gestured to the pile of papers in an angry way and threw her hands in the air before turning abruptly away and going back upstairs.

He did not look any better for this meeting. A shadow crossed his face as he took up one of the bills and set it down again in frustration and took up another.

An idea had occurred to Sandra. Though it didn't look hopeful, she would ask for employment. She pushed in the door. He did not notice her approach as he sipped tea and read a letter.

"If you please, sir," she began. He looked up. His eyes were dark and troubled. He hardly seemed to see her at first, and then he frowned.

"What is it?" he snapped.

What a rude manner he has, thought Sandra. It was very unpromising. But she was in no position to walk away. Still, her heart dropped. Another brick wall awaited. How many more?

"I'm looking for work, sir. I wonder if—"

He flicked his eyes upward, with impatience there, cutting her off.

"It's not that kind of Gentleman's Club," he snapped.

She didn't get his meaning.

"Not that kind of—?"

"Not that kind of club we run here!" his eyes fixed on her, before he realised that he might have misunderstood. Those large green eyes seemed not to understand. She had an accent. His manner softened.

"You must be new here. It's very dangerous for you at the moment, you know? There's a murderer on the loose. He has targeted women such as you."

Sandra was close to tears, but she held herself in a dignified way.

"Such as me, sir? You are not running that sort of club, sir, and I'm not that sort of girl. I am a cook. I was going to offer you my services as a cook." She blinked back tears.

"Oh, I beg your pardon, Miss." his remorse seemed genuine. He shuffled some papers. "As it happens, we are in need of a cook. How much experience do you have?"

"Four years, sir, in a gentleman's home."

"May I see your references?" he asked.

There it was again.

"I am sorry, sir, I have no references."

"Tha's unusual. Might I enquire why not?"

"You may, sir, and I will tell you. I left my former position in great haste, because I was in immediate danger from my employer, who importuned me, and was not about to take *No* for an answer." She blushed furiously. She hardly believed that she had said it. But she was sick to death of being turned away. Perhaps she should have told the truth in the houses she had applied to, instead of being vague. "I ran out of his house, sir, made for the railway station, caught a train that was leaving that moment, and here I am in London, in great need of a situation."

She had his full attention now. He put down his papers.

"I say, that's a dreadful thing to happen. Won't you sit down? Take some tea. Whistler! Bring another cup!"

Sandra sat down, hardly believing that she was not out on the street again.

"I'm sorry I was less than polite just now, and for misunderstanding your situation." he said, gesturing to the papers as if they told their own story.

"That's all right."

"You're from the North, aren't you? I can tell by your accent."

"Yes, sir. Yorkshire."

"And you wanted to get as far away as you could from this—this employer you had."

"I thought I'd try my chances in London, but I'm finding it very difficult to get a position without references."

He poured her a cup of tea. Then he took his own tea and sat back in a rather relaxed way. She felt his eyes examine her closely, trying to make out her character, she supposed. Or perhaps he was looking at her awful hat, though the canary-yellow ribbon was an improvement.

"Tell me more about your culinary skills. Where did you learn?"

She told him how she had been taught by the cook, where there was a great deal of entertaining due to the employer's prominent position in the town, and that for three years she had been in charge of the kitchen.

"But what can you cook?" he asked with eagerness.

"Plain, everyday family dinners as well as French dishes and desserts, for the cook who trained me was proficient in those. I've worked mostly on my own, but I have cooked for as many as twenty at table, with outside help brought in."

"Can you cook me something for my lunch?"

Sandra suddenly relaxed and laughed. He had asked like one of her brothers would.

"I would be happy to, sir."

"Whistler!" the man appeared again from the back.

"This is Mrs.—?"

"Oh, I'm a Miss, and may be called so," said Sandra warmly. She had no time for the custom of calling a cook Mrs. to give her extra maturity. "I'm not quite ready to be Mrs.!"

He seemed to think that amusing and smiled. She thought him very handsome when he smiled, he had a broad clear forehead, and his eyes were kind.

"My name is Sandra Boone."

"I am Clement Lark," he said. They shook hands.

"Thank you for giving me a chance, Mr. Lark. I won't disappoint you. What would you like for lunch?"

"What's in there, Whistler?"

"There's a chicken, just killed this morning. I have to go to the market for beef and eels and vegetables."

"Can you cook *coque au vin?*" he asked. "For two, as my mother will join me."

"Yes, I can. Are there onions, carrots, and thyme? Fresh thyme?" she wheeled around to ask Whistler.

"I do believe those items are in stock, Miss. But no coke."

"Coke?"

"We had a misunderstanding this morning, Miss Boone. I mentioned *coque au vin*, and Mr. Whistler thought it was chicken charred on coke from coal."

"Oh, I see. No, it's begun on the range and then I like to finish it off in the oven. It tastes better that way. And wine—Burgundy is best."

He hesitated.

"Burgundy is expensive, Miss Boone."

"I can use a cheaper wine—there are no strict rules. Every cook has to adapt the ingredients to the budget. And—what's leftover today, can be something else for tomorrow."

"We will have Burgundy today," Clement declared.

"Oh, and if you have any mushrooms, they will add interest!" Sandra followed Whistler back to the kitchen. The kitchen was large and—good!—a modern gas range! She donned an apron with great hope and anticipation. She asked for a sharp knife and cutting board and got to work. Soon, a delicious aroma of chicken cooking in wine and herbs filled the hall. New to this particular oven, she tested and sampled often. She set the dish before Mr. Lark and his mother an hour later, and watched them surreptitiously from the kitchen door. She was pleased to see him dig into the food, but was he relishing it? His mother ate thoughtfully at first, but appeared to approve as she went on. For dessert, she'd whipped up a meringue.

"That was perfect, Miss Boone. Can you begin immediately?" asked Mr. Lark, smiling with eagerness.

"Yes, sir."

"I don't know how many to expect tonight, will you manage, do you think?"

"Yes, sir, but—I will need some help eventually, if you are accustomed to being busy. Mr. Whistler tells me he doesn't rightly belong in kitchen, and waits at table."

"What do you need?" he asked.

"A kitchen maid, or two preferably, if the food is to be upon the plates in a timely manner."

"I will advertise straight away. As to your wages—how does thirty pounds a year sound? You will work six nights a week. I will advance you a sum as you're new in London. I know a respectable lodging-house a short distance away in Witley Street. I will pay for your lodgings. I'm sorry you cannot stay here, at least not at the moment. My mother occupies the housekeeper's room when she visits, and the servants' quarters are not at all suitable for habitation just now."

She was so happy she could have cried.

"Clement," she heard his mother whisper. "Are you sure about her?"

"Mother, that luncheon was the best I have ever eaten! What can go amiss?"

CHAPTER TWENTY-FOUR

S he began that very evening. But to her great dismay, and everybody's amusement, she had no idea what *eel pie 'n mas* was—what sort of pie—potatoes like shepherd's pie, or was it in a pastry base? She'd never cooked eel. The Thames, she was told, was teeming with the creatures.

"Even I know how to cook pie 'n mash," Mr. Lark said with some amusement. "The sauce or liquor has to be made from the water the eels were stewed in, and you add plenty of parsley to turn it green. I'll write it out for you. Whistler, stop looking as if you have seen a pig fly. The British Empire is vast, and what's commonplace here may not be so in other districts, not even in other parts of England."

"Oh, I know, sir. I do like a curry, myself." Whistler left the kitchen to polish the bar.

"Here's the recipe, have a shot at it. We'll put *coque au vin* and shepherd's pie on the menu too."

"I saved the egg yolks from the meringue, to make a béarnaise sauce to liven up any plain dish, Mr. Lark. It will keep for a few days."

"That's good, Miss Boone."

But there were only three dinner orders that evening, two for pie 'n mash and one shepherd's pie.

Wondering why there had been so few, she peered out into the hall. There were only five gentlemen there, and two of them must have eaten elsewhere.

Mr. Lark walked Sandra back to her lodgings. She'd been up very early that morning and she was, at midnight, very tired now, but utterly happy. She felt that she'd found her own little bit of London at The Oakes Gentlemen's Club.

Mr. Lark told her he had already submitted advertisements for help in the kitchen. Sandra wondered if there would really be enough work for a kitchen maid, after she had said she would need two!

She had to do her utmost to do him proud, to cook not just well, but superbly, for she didn't want to go job-hunting again in one week!

CHAPTER TWENTY-FIVE

G ladys Knave started work as a kitchen maid the following Monday. She was a very pretty, sharpish girl who bristled when given orders, and though a fast and efficient worker, Sandra did not take to her. She seemed resentful in some way. She much preferred Lillian Coolidge, a chatty girl with rosy cheeks who began two days after that, as between-maid, working as needed between the kitchen and making beds upstairs, for the Club had accommodation. Business had picked up a little, and her shepherd's pie, for all its simplicity, was popular.

To Mr. Lark's satisfaction two gentlemen came in one night and ordered *coq au vin*. They pronounced it excellent and sent their compliments to the chef. Before they left, Mr. Lark discovered that they were regulars at an exclusive club in town but happened to investigate Whitechapel to see for themselves what it was like and if there was any decent place for a gentleman who did not want raucous entertainment or vice. Mr. Lark was full of glee as he strode into the kitchen.

"Imagine them going back to White's and saying, '*We found this little gem in the East End. It's called The Oakes—authentic*

Tudor, with modern conveniences. The owner, a fellow named Lark, told us it's locally very popular. You should go down and give it a try, Gentlemen. We had superb fare and the wine was excellent.'"

Sandra laughed at his mischievous imaginings.

"Mr. Lark, did you really tell them that this Club was very popular locally?" she asked as she spooned left-over vegetables into a bowl.

"Of course! I told them that they'd come on a quiet night, that most people had gone to a concert in London Fields."

"And—have they?"

"How would I know? Just because I did not see a playbill doesn't mean there wasn't one. There may be."

"You mean Spitalfield, sir? That's just a common!" laughed Lillian. Gladys was scrubbing a pot and glared at her for the nerve of taking part in a conversation between Mr. Lark and his cook. Anyway, Miss Boone wasn't as good a cook as all that either. She was just showing off, and if you poured wine into a pot along with onions and flavourings, people don't notice if the meat is gone off. She knew that trick. And Miss Boone talked funny, leaving out *'the'* and *'a'* before words. Today she'd ordered her to *get carrots and scrub them.* It should have been *the carrots.* That was no way to speak the Queen's English. Gladys resented having to take orders from somebody from up North who didn't speak proper English.

When she went off that evening, she'd tell Timothy what a rotten job this was. Even Lillian got on her nerves. She was plump and silly and laughed too much.

The gentlemen returned the following week, and brought six friends, and Clement and his mother were very pleased indeed.

CHAPTER TWENTY-SIX

Dear Sandra,
  It was so great to hear from you and to get your remittance, it was very welcome, I went out and bought ingredients for bread & butter pudding & baked a filling dinner. Your employer sounds like a good man. A bachelor you say, but you did not write if he was handsome! Mamma is the same. She eats very little. Papa is still at the mill. How he endures it, I don't know. I can only assume that it would be worse for him at home all day with Mamma. He really cannot bear to see her so melancholic. What a horrible disease melancholia is and there's nothing to be done except strong medicaments that send her faraway in her mind. She laments often that her daughters have no pretty things as she had. Our John began at the Ragged School and does well. Eliza has a mind of her own, she takes after Aunt Maud, same eyes and all. Have you seen our Stevie yet?

The letter went on with news about neighbours and people they knew. Anna hadn't said a word about herself though. Unselfish Anna! Sandra felt guilty that it was she who had escaped. But Anna would never leave their mother as long as she was needed. Once again, Sandra felt the familiar hopelessness about her mother's mental state. She missed her family very much, but looked forward to a trip to Hove.

Before long, she heard from the Knightleys. They'd been overjoyed to find her letter when they returned from Europe. Could she come and visit them next Sunday? She set out on the train which brought her through the Sussex countryside, and at Hove Station she was met by them, and by her brother, now thirteen and grown tall. Stevie held his hand out to her in a polite greeting.

"Why Stevie, no hug for your big sister then?" she chided him as she bestowed a kiss on his forehead. He looked at her as if she were a stranger, and it pierced her heart.

The Knightley house was an elegant three-storey in a quiet street. They ate their Sunday dinner in the dining room and in speaking about her family in Skipton, Sandra was conscious that Stevie, though listening, was reserved, as if she spoke of strangers.

"You remember your brother, John," she addressed him. "He's attending school."

"Will he join me at King Edward's?" he asked.

"No, he will learn a trade."

"Oh." Stevie's eyes betrayed his lack of understanding.

"But he wants to be a train driver." Sandra said then, and her brother's eyes lit up.

"I say, I do too!"

From then on, he was chatty, no longer a stranger, and they talked easily as they walked the promenade as far as Brighton until it was time to leave for her train.

CHAPTER TWENTY-SEVEN

"**B**usiness seems to be picking up," observed Mrs. Lark. "Ten clients tonight, and two are staying. But it's not enough, Clement."

"Mother, August is a month people do not like to be in Town." Clement wolfed his roast beef and Yorkshire pudding. "This is first-rate."

"I grant you she's a good cook," said his mother, watching him.

"She's also a very nice lady." The moment Clement had said it, he knew it was a mistake.

"Hardly a lady, Clement."

"You know what I meant, Mother."

"Clement, you don't harbour any intentions, do you? Because you are never going to marry a servant, no matter how well she cooks."

"Oh no, Mother!" Clement meant what he said, yet he was taken back to his first meeting with Miss Boone, and her clear skin and wide green eyes that swam with tears at his rudeness, and he felt a tenderness for her.

"So, she's from Yorkshire." His mother added, probably prodding him to say more.

"From Skipton. A town not far from Leeds, I believe."

"What was her father's trade?"

"In truth, I do not know. Perhaps a butler or something."

Unknown to Mrs. Lark, she had piqued Clement's curiosity about the tall girl with green eyes that he had just employed. He was in the habit of discussing the menu with her every evening. Perhaps tonight he'd broach the subject of her family.

Sandra had decided to tell the truth if asked about her or her family's past, so when Mr. Lark asked her if she had heard from her people in the North, she said that she had, and expanded this by saying that her parents were in poor health.

"Your father is unable to work then?"

"He works, but it's an undemanding job as secretary to—a mill owner, Mr. Grant. Before that, he was a country squire with a large farm."

"I say!" Clement showed his astonishment.

Sandra went on to relate the great misfortune that had befallen the family. He listened with rapt attention.

"I—I had no idea!" he stammered. "What a fiend that man must have been! Is there not any redress, none at all?"

"None. He got away, and it wouldn't surprise me if he is again in a position of trust somewhere else."

"Good gracious. Such a person as that should not be allowed to be free."

They discussed the next day's menu, and Clement walked away, his head full of the story he had heard. What an astonishing, tragic history! What a brave girl she was! Miss Boone soared in his estimation. He was deep in thought for the rest of the night.

CHAPTER TWENTY-EIGHT

"Timothy, why can't you tell me where you're going?"

Gladys was upset. She loved Timothy Bright. She used to think that he loved her too, now she wasn't sure. He was cagey, was Timothy. He played his cards close to his chest.

"I 'ave to meet a friend, who wants me to put someone up for a time. I'm bringin' 'im back here."

"Here! But where will this someone sleep?"

"He won't be too fussy about the accommodation. He'll be glad of any place to while away a few weeks."

"A few weeks! That's too much, Timothy, without asking me first."

"Who pays the rent 'ere, Gladys?"

"You do."

"There you are."

"And who gets everything free without 'aving to buy a girl a ring?"

"I'd marry you if I could, Gladys. I told you that, didn't I? Trouble is, I got a wife. Now be a sweet girl and kiss me before I go."

"I'm afeard to stay here on my own, after the murder in George's Yard. I heard it was vicious and horrible."

"It's safe as 'ouses here, Gladys. And doesn't your boss walk you 'ome?"

"No, I tell 'im my brother comes to take me home. I don't want 'im to know my private life. I come home by myself. He walks the others home but he's talkin' about gettin' someone to do it so 'e can stay at the Club."

"Does he 'ave anybody yet?"

"No."

"Maybe I'll put in for it. It sounds like an easy way to earn a few bob."

"Really, Tim?"

"Really, Gladys. I know him, remember, from the time I used to work for his uncle."

"But 'is uncle sacked you."

"He doesn't know that, does he? I'll tell him I worked for his uncle for five years and left of my own accord to start my tanning business. Which failed."

"You 'aven't got a reference, you silly man."

"Oh yes, I do 'ave a reference. It's not mine strickly speaking, but it will be. A glowing reference. Before I left, I managed to pry open the cabinet and I nicked a few letters of his, with his signature."

"You'd have to walk Miss Boone home too. You wouldn't like that. She's bossy and stuffy and talks funny. And Lillian prattles on about 'er cat and 'er budgie, and—well, I 'ope the cat eats the budgie. I am sick of her."

"It's orright. I'm equal to the task. Well, I'm off."

He kissed her goodbye and left. She heard his footsteps clatter on the stairs and going to the window, watched him across the street.

She wished she could be sure of him.

CHAPTER TWENTY-NINE

The following morning, Gladys woke to find a strange man sleeping in their living room, in the one armchair by the fireplace. She examined him with a cynical eye while he slept. He was bony, with dark hair, and a thin, unhealthy face.

I suppose he'll expect me to cook for 'im! And where's Timothy? She would get dressed quickly and go out to work early before this stranger woke up.

She was successful in leaving the small flat unnoticed. Timothy was coming up the street.

"I went to see Mr. Lark. I said I was looking for a job, part-time, showed 'im the references. I got it! And he doesn't even know we know each other so don't look all starry-eyed when I appear tonight to walk you 'ome."

"That was quick work. Your friend is still asleep in the living room. What's his name?"

"I don't know really. He tells me it's Silas Greenway. Don't go on when I tell you 'e smokes opium and snuffs cocaine. Tha's why 'e has that twitch of 'is."

"What's his business?"

He put a finger over her lips.

"Ask no questions, Gladys, and you'll be told no lies."

"I don't like it, Timothy!"

"Don't worry, my pet. He's 'armless. He's just a brain and never gets 'is hands dirty. See you tonight, then."

Gladys had to keep her romance secret because Mrs. Lark disapproved of "followers." It was enough to get a girl sacked. How was the next generation to be born, if servants weren't allowed romance and marriage? Not that she could marry Timothy. He'd told her he was married the third time they'd met. She'd been disappointed, but continued to meet him, and then she'd accepted his invitation to live with him. It wasn't uncommon in the East End. A girl just had to make the best of it. Nobody in the Club knew that she'd known Mr. Bright before he began to escort them home. He went to Witley Street first with Miss Boone and Lillian, and then came back for her, ostensibly to lead her to a lodging in Cramden Court.

She came in one night after a particularly difficult day, to find, as usual, their "guest" in the chair nearest the fire. He didn't talk a lot, this pale, boring man. But as she came in, she burst out: "Am I glad to get home, Miss Boone didn't half get on my nerves today! Fussed at me about the carrots again. Said I cut them too small for the pot. I am sick to death of her."

"Miss Boone?"

"Yes, Miss Boone. I am sick to death of her. I wish she'd stayed up in the North."

"She's not from London, then? She's from—?" His chin twitched.

"The North. Yorkshire or someplace. She can't speak proper English."

Her guest thought before he spoke again.

"What's her Christian name?"

"It's Sandra. Why, do you know her?"

He made no reply. He got up and walked about the room. It made Gladys uneasy.

"When does Timothy get home?" he asked her abruptly.

"I don't know. He dropped me off at the door and said 'e had to see someone."

"Where does Miss Boone stay?"

"Oh, Witley Street. Why do you want to know? You know Miss Boone?"

"No, I don't."

"You're lying. You do."

"If I tell you something, will you promise not to tell anybody?"

"Orright."

"Her brother is a crook, who I had occasion to cross paths with, once. I have never forgotten it."

"In London, or in the North?"

"It's best to say no more about the subject, Miss."

"You 'ave secrets, don't you?"

CHAPTER THIRTY

August had not gone by when the news of another murder of an unfortunate woman, this time in Buck's Row, seized Whitechapel. This was a vicious killing and everyone who heard of it was revolted beyond belief. The newspapers began to take notice that these murders were related and reporters swarmed all over Whitechapel.

Sandra looked out the window and saw policemen everywhere, and photographers and reporters among them, interviewing people, taking notes and photos. There was an air of fear among everybody. But customers poured in looking for something to eat. In some clubs, you had to be a member to enter, but here, Mr. Lark was so anxious to build up his business that he was welcoming everybody he could. Suddenly, the kitchen was very busy.

"Is it right that we benefit from this horrible thing?" she wondered aloud.

"Your sentiment is a noble one, Miss Boone, but hungry people have to eat." Mrs. Lark was just behind her. "I came in to see if you were all right, as it is so busy. I can don an apron and stir a sauce, or watch something for you, if you like."

"That's very kind of you, Mrs. Lark, but we're managing very well. Gladys mashes the potatoes until she gets that lovely creamy texture you see there, and Lillian is everywhere helping."

Mrs. Lark gave a smile and a look of approval all-round before she left.

That wasn't too bad of Miss Boone, thought Gladys, pleased. *Maybe she's not so bad after all.*

CHAPTER THIRTY-ONE

The club buzzed with conversation and there were some chairs designated for those who were waiting to be seated for dinner. Mrs. Lark became hostess and greeted the men coming in and seated them, while her son hovered about the tables, helped to manage the bar and took the dinner orders. Whistler served at table, and pleased he was at all the tips coming his way.

A group of reporters from The London Leader sat at one table, comparing notes. Clement was nearby when he overheard an interesting exchange.

"I suppose this will push your International Crime Investigation to the back page, Staunton."

"Yes, if it gets published at all."

"What story is that?" asked another reporter.

"There's a swindler operating in Europe and the United Kingdom. His name is Craven but he has several aliases. He was almost arrested in Europe some years ago and then came here, where he secured a position as steward to an unfortunate farmer named Boone, in Yorkshire, an ailing man with a young family. He ruined them. He skipped to the Continent again, but he's back here in England, said to be in London now, and my sources tell me he's in Whitechapel."

The subject changed back to the murders, but Clement took note of the reporter—a ginger-haired man with spectacles, so that he could find him again.

"Whistler," he said. "You see that man? Don't allow him to leave without speaking with me."

"Very good, guv'nor."

Some time later he was talking to Mr. Staunton in a more private area of the Club.

"It's vital you find that scoundrel," Mr. Lark said. "I personally know one of the Boone family. If Craven's in Whitechapel, I'd like to know."

"I've had to suspend my investigation, Mr. Lark, in the light of the Whitechapel Murders. Not that this Craven man isn't a murderer too, mind you. There was a suspicious death in Gibraltar and he fled. It's said one of his victims in Switzerland found out where he was and followed him to have him arrested. The man disappeared. He fell off a cliff."

This information made Mr. Lark very concerned. What if Mr. Craven saw Miss Boone? It could place her in danger. Would he recognise her though, as a woman grown? She would surely know *him*.

"What does this man Craven look like?"

"Unfortunately, like a lot of men. Average looks, dark-haired, medium height, thin. He never allows a photograph. He is said to have a facial twitch. Otherwise, a non-descript appearance. His accent changes wherever he finds himself. He blends in well. I must be off, Mr. Lark, they're waiting for me. Get in touch if you have any new information."

He disappeared after his colleagues who had already exited the Club.

Clement wondered whether to tell Sandra. To think that the evil man who beggared her family was within reach, if only they could find him!

"Clement, you must be pleased with this evening's business," remarked his mother as he locked the doors. She had taken up almost permanent residence there now.

"I suppose so, Mother. But it's because of a brutal murder."

"I understand," she said. "Life throws you some very odd turns sometimes. It's very good of you to feel as you do, Clement, but don't let it gnaw at you."

"No, Mother," he managed a weak smile and walked away. His mother had no idea of the other matter that was on his mind.

He agonised for hours about whether he should let Sandra know. What was likely to happen if he did? She would want to look for Craven. She would become restless, and perhaps go out into the streets herself, searching. He would not be able to stop her. There was no point in her going to the police and expecting them to find this man who had swindled her family. Every man in the City of London and the Metropolitan Police was focused on one crime—finding the man named Jack the Ripper.

He felt a heavy responsibility. Could he look her in the eye, knowing he was keeping this information from her? He could not make the decision with the hard-headed attitude of an employer about his employee. Sandra could despise him if he did not tell her this. That was the very last thing Clement Lark wanted to happen!

But he'd have to risk it.

CHAPTER THIRTY-TWO

Gladys had made up her mind. She was leaving Timothy. The visitor's odd manners frightened her. He spent his days at the table with stacks of papers in front of him, writing names over and over. He sniffed the white powder and told her once that he could see her from the ceiling, when he was actually in the chair opposite. She did not sleep a wink if Tim was not present. Cocaine had made the stranger a madman. Silas was waiting for word from the Continent about a boat which would take him away from England, and she didn't know when that would come, if ever.

Tim was the other reason she was leaving. Gladys was not content to continue with this existence of being his woman —no vows, no promises, no ring, and their children would be looked down upon and have no chances in life. And she'd seen him make eyes at silly Lillian, of all people!

"Miss Boone, could you ask Mrs. Smithson if there's a vacancy at Witley Street?" she asked Sandra one day. Sandra was surprised, but complied with the request, and unknown to Timothy, a few mornings later Gladys gathered her few belongings and moved. She didn't much like living under the same roof as Miss Boone and Lillian, but Mr. Lark was paying. Miss Boone was all right most of the time now, but Lillian got on her nerves. That cat! She could hear the two of them arguing sometimes about the cat.

Timothy wouldn't be able to make a scene as she didn't see him on his own now. He simply scowled when he came in the first evening to escort the three ladies back to their lodgings.

"I wonder if there's any need for *your services* now, Mr. Bright." said Gladys airily as she donned her little pert hat. "We are three of us now. If any of us meets Leather Apron, or whatever they are calling the murderer now, I daresay say we can clobber him." He glowered, his face a dark shadow, and Sandra, who saw the exchange, knew there had been something between them. She still did not like Timothy Bright.

CHAPTER THIRTY-THREE

"So, the girl is gone?" Silas seemed to be more concerned than Timothy that Gladys had absconded.

"Yep. I'm not going to worry about it. I'm not so attached as to go after her. She was clingy. I knew that from the first, so I told 'er I was married."

Silas paced up and down the small room, his hands in his pockets, a frown furrowing his face.

"Would you stop that walking? You're makin' me nervous. Whassup w' you?"

"Gladys fell out with you. She won't be loyal to you anymore now, will she? She'll betray me."

"Oh, Gladys knows noffink about your activities, nor mine." Tim dismissed the thought with a wave of his hand.

"She's living under the same roof as Miss Boone. They may well become friends, and talk, as women do. Soon, Gladys will disclose that Timothy Bright has a man staying in his flat who knew her in Yorkshire, and that this man is waiting for a craft from France to come and take him out of the country. Perhaps she will add that this man does not wish to be discovered by police. Miss Boone is intelligent and bold with it; she'll tumble to it that Silas Greenway may well be another man known to her."

"You crossed swords with her brother up in Yorkshire? Was it that bad then?"

"It was something more than that. I will put it like this, quite plainly. I have to be sure Miss Boone does not know anything about my presence here or, that she doesn't even have any opportunity to find out. I'm very serious and I will be prepared to pay handsomely to get rid of her."

"What are you sayin'?"

"As King Henry said, *'Will no one rid me of this troublesome priest?'*"

"I'm not interested in history."

"In the year 1170, King Henry the Second was tired of Archbishop Thomas Becket, and when he asked that question, he was really asking—"

"I'm not stupid, mate. I know what he was askin'. I know what you're askin'. I don't know about this, Silas. You better make it worth my while, then. I do 'ave contacts. It will take some days to get this going."

"Just one more requirement," Craven said. "Could you, after it's done, and she's found, put it about the streets that her employer Clement Lark is this Jack the Ripper fellow?"

"You get the oddest ideas, but orright, if that's what you want."

Everything was quiet for some days in the East End, and business was beginning to be consistently good. Clement was falling in love with Sandra. The more he thought of her tragic situation, her bravery and how she obviously denied herself to send money to her family, the more he admired her. Even his mother was coming to like her quite well. She even gave her one of her cast-off hats, which was still a very good hat, a neat fashionable forest green toque with sprightly white feathers. She looked queenly in it, much better than his mother had ever looked in it. It matched her lovely eyes. But everything she wore, Mr. Lark thought, she wore it well.

Sandra was very pleased with the hat, and put it by for Sunday.

CHAPTER THIRTY-FOUR

"Oooh Miss Boone! Miss Boone! Please come quickly!"

What was wrong with Lillian Coolidge? She was banging on the door at seven o'clock in the morning. As they worked late, they didn't get up until late. Sandra jumped out of bed.

"Oooh Miss Boone! You won't believe it! Come quickly! Gladys! Come and see!" Lillian had moved on to Gladys' door and banged hard upon it, and Sandra heard a very cross Gladys snap that unless the Queen was downstairs, she wasn't getting up.

Sandra wrapped a shawl around her shoulders and followed Lillian. The room was typical Lillian, colourful and chaotic.

"It's Algernon, my cat! He's not a boy after all! He's a mother now. When I came in last night, I threw my hat in the corner behind the bed, I know it's a bad thing to do to a hat, but little did I know it would be a nursery this morning!" sang Lillian, as her visitor peered in the darkness toward a cat and three newborn mewling kittens, all curled together in Lillian's bright feathery hat.

"I told you, Lillian, that Algernon was a girl. I told you I grew up on a farm and could tell when a cat was about to have a family. You didn't believe me until now!"

"Oooh Miss Boone, yes, you did say that! But the people who gave her to me swore to me he was a boy! How can I call her Algernon now? I'll have to change her name! And so clever, to choose my hat! They look so cosy there, I shan't disturb them. Oooh my goodness, Miss Boone, I have no hat now, what shall I do? I can't go out without a hat!"

"Do you want to wear mine? I have another, a better one. My brown is not at all nice, but it would do you for a time. And Lillian, good luck to your cat and her little family, but you didn't have to wake me at this hour."

"Ooooh but I couldn't wait, Miss Boone! I was that excited! Shall I come and get your hat now, so's not to disturb you later? I have to go out and buy food for my little cat, I think she could murder a nice chop, don't you?"

"Oh, don't spend money on a chop when she'd just as soon eat a bit of offal the butcher is going to throw out," said Sandra. "And will Mrs. Smithson let you keep them? Where's your budgie?"

"I gave him away, it wasn't fair, him living in fear all day of Algernon."

"I'll say it wasn't fair, Lillian. I told you that as well. I'm glad you took my advice at last. Come on, I'll give you my old hat now. It's horrid but it's better than no hat at all."

CHAPTER THIRTY-FIVE

It was getting on for eleven, time to go to work, and Lillian had not come back. Sandra went out the front door, looked up and down the street for her. Gladys did not like to walk with them to work and had set off by herself a little earlier.

Sandra grew uneasy. The butcher's shop was only a few streets away, but there was a shortcut down a narrow alley, which was often deserted. She hadn't warned Lillian to go the longer route, and now chided herself. Lillian often did not think.

She wondered if she should go to the butcher's and enquire if she had been there, but it was getting late, and she decided to go to work instead and let Mr. Lark know that she was concerned. Perhaps Lillian, in her excitement over the kittens, had forgotten to wait for her and just gone ahead. Maybe she was at work already.

She reached the club, but Lillian was not there. Mr. Lark was concerned enough to send out for Mr. Bright.

Sandra was in the kitchen when she heard the doors open and Mr. Lark's voice raised in greeting as Mr. Bright entered the Club. She put down the saucepan she'd taken out for the soup and came hurrying out, intending to give him the details of where Lillian had gone that morning.

But Mr. Bright stopped dead in his tracks when he saw her. She saw him blink twice, then an expression of something like horror crossed his eyes, and his face turn pale. He seemed to freeze.

"Are you well, Mr. Bright?" asked Clement, as Sandra withdrew into the kitchen, afraid, wondering what it meant. What a very odd reaction! She kept the door a little open, so that she could hear.

"Yes Guv'nor. Quite well enough." He spoke faster than normal.

"All right then, here's the situation. Miss Coolidge went missing this morning," began Clement briskly. "It may be a very innocent explanation—she went to the butchers and may have gone somewhere else for something also. Perhaps she forgot the time. In light of what's been happening here in Whitechapel, I'd like you to go and look for her."

"Yes, Guv'nor." His voice sounded weak and hoarse.

"Go to her lodgings, go to the butchers—Moores on Brick Street—and find people who saw her this morning. And if you find her dilly-dallying somewhere, remind her it's not her day off and to get herself in here as fast as she can. Come back in one hour. No later. If you can't find her in the hour, we need to go to the police, with all that's been happening here, I'm not going to take a chance."

Sandra could not resist peering out again. Mr. Bright hurried away almost before Mr. Lark had finished speaking. She went back to resume her work, frowning, wondering about him. Gladys was in the scullery scouring pots.

After the doors banged shut behind him, Mrs. Lark came downstairs.

"Clement," she said in a very urgent tone. "There is something very odd about that man. I was standing at the top of the stairs, and he stopped dead in the middle of the floor, looking toward the back of the Hall, as if he had seen a ghost. What could he have seen?"

"I do not know, Mother. I noticed he seemed perturbed at something or other."

"I shall ask Gladys and Miss Boone if they passed and saw anything odd." She swept away.

Clement got up from his seat and paced about. Something was wrong, he felt it. Mr. Bright had unnerved his mother, the very practical, level-headed woman who was not given to silly fears and imaginings. If his mother was concerned, he ought to be.

His mother returned to find him in front of the fireplace, deep in thought.

"Miss Boone saw him." she said. "She heard the front door and came out to give her account of this morning. She saw his very odd reaction, and withdrew. She is quite perturbed at it. Clement, what is the matter?"

Her son had begun to pace the floor with briskness and agitation.

"Oh, Mother," he said, covering his head in his hands. "I feel that Miss Boone may be in great danger. If I'm right, then Lillian—poor Lillian! I hope I'm wrong, 'oh God!'" he prayed.

"I hope I'm wrong. Why did I not act? Why did I not tell her?"

"Of what are you talking, son?" his mother sounded annoyed. She did not like mysteries. But Clement did not answer her. He had swept past her, into the kitchen.

CHAPTER THIRTY-SIX

S andra swirled the onions, carrots, and parsnips around in a sizzling pool of lard and covered the saucepan tightly, with a cotton cloth wedged under the lid, to sweat them. She ran her hands down her apron. Her mind was on Timothy Bright. His demeanour, his expression, was imprinted in her mind and it made her very uneasy. Timothy had not expected to see her.

The door burst open, and Mr. Lark stood there, his face red, dark eyes wide, his hair tousled, uneasiness almost convulsing his frame.

"Miss Boone," he said. "I must speak with you as a matter of exigency. Be so good as to come into the hall."

"Of course, sir." Sandra's fear mounted at his words, especially the formality of his speech. "Gladys?" she called out. "Watch vegetables, will you? Don't let them burn in fat!"

"Yes, Miss Boone." came Gladys's answer from the scullery. Sandra did not hear *"the* vegetables, *the* fat," that the girl muttered to herself.

Mr. Lark looked desperate as he looked about him.

"Where's Whistler?"

"You gave him the morning off to go to the dentist," said his mother. "What's the matter with you, Clement?"

Mr. Lark groaned and ran out the front door. He returned after a few minutes.

"Miss Boone, I am desperately worried about Miss Coolidge. I have just dispatched our neighbour to fetch a policeman. My mother saw Mr. Bright's reaction when he saw you. And you noted it too. *As if he had seen a ghost*, my mother put it." He paused.

"There—there is something I should have told you some time ago," he stammered. "Please sit down."

"What is this, Clement?" his mother seated herself also.

"What was the name of the man who swindled your father?" he asked.

"It was Mr. Craven."

"A journalist with The Leader told me that he is here, in Whitechapel."

Sandra gasped and rose from the table abruptly.

"Where? Where? Tell me!"

"He did not know. He was investigating it and then was removed from that story to cover the Whitechapel Murders. Is there any way, Miss Boone, that this Mr. Craven might know you are here in Whitechapel?"

Sandra shook her head. "I can't think of any. I doubt if he'd know me now, for I was only a girl when we last met. He wouldn't know unless somebody had mentioned my name to him, but I'm only known to the people here, and to Mrs. Smithson."

A thought struck her.

"Mr. Lark, I often felt there was a connection between Gladys and Timothy Bright. Of a romantic nature. And that they had a falling-out recently. I don't know what that might have to do with all this unless Mr. Bright and Mr. Craven know each other."

"Is there any way that perhaps Lillian might have been mistaken for you this morning?" Clement hated to ask the question and dreaded the implication.

A smell of burning fat reached them from the back. Sandra got up and ran back to the kitchen, took a kitchen towel and pulled the smoking pot off the gasfire. "Gladys! Gladys! Where are you?"

But there was no sign of Gladys in the kitchen, the scullery, or the pantry. Her hat was gone from the hook in the back hall. Sandra returned to the front.

"Now could somebody enlighten me as to the swindling and all that was mentioned between you and Miss Boone just now?" Mrs. Lark was demanding to know.

Clement cast her a glance, and she nodded. Why keep it a secret? This was urgent.

CHAPTER THIRTY-SEVEN

M r. Craven was disturbed and very angry. He did not like anything going wrong, and it had. He always planned everything perfectly, and was always well upon his way before his crime was found. He never had to see the consequences of his actions and never even thought about them.

He liked his crimes to be clean and never wanted to see a victim's face. He abhorred pained, angry countenances. Yet, because they had encountered an emergency this morning and there was nobody else, he was supposed to watch over the middle-aged woman until Bright returned. It was distasteful to see a woman tied up and with a gag over her mouth, looking at him with hateful, accusing eyes, though he had assured her that he never had hurt a woman in his life, and that she'd be quite free to go in a few hours as soon as the plan was in place.

It was a bad coincidence that his arrival here had coincided with the Whitechapel Murders and that the place was swarming with police. It was a truly dreadful coincidence that the Boone girl had turned up near the place where he was hiding.

He couldn't show his face in Wiltshire again; his family had disowned him. After the Yorkshire incident, which they all knew of, they'd called him a bad seed and he supposed that he was, though he remembered a time when he was a good person. That was when he was younger. He'd been a good, churchgoing boy, the son of a gentleman farmer, comfortable but not rich. What had happened to throw him on this path?

He had an unusual ability for numbers, and at the age of eighteen he had been introduced to real wealth. He'd seen it as tutor to the son of Lord and Lady Calderon. He saw beautiful, expensive things everywhere in their grand house and he wanted the same. He wanted to be rich. It became a consuming desire. How could he become rich? He could not marry money—he knew he wasn't handsome or charming enough to win an heiress. Work would never reward him with anything like the level of wealth he craved. He concluded he'd have to use his brain and his superior mathematical acumen to win himself riches, and he prided himself on an acting ability to make himself appear honest, good, and trustworthy. It was the only way, he had argued with himself. He was a superior being in a low position in the world. It should not have been like that. Life had been unfair to him and he was justified in taking what he always felt should be his.

He'd started small, and far away from home. He'd gone to the Continent and become friends with a number of English people in Switzerland and offered his services to wealthy families. This gave him access to private documents and soon he was able to practice signatures. He was an excellent forger, and was making quite a lot of money, which he used to support his expensive tastes and his liking for cocaine. He disliked company, although he had to attend parties to become introduced to prospects. All he wanted was a grand solitude in a large house, with as few servants as possible, a few chosen friends, fine wines, a large collection of art and money to count.

But his luck had run out in Switzerland and he had been discovered. He'd gone to Paris, but word had got there before him. There wasn't much to do in Paris, and he was aware that he'd been looked at like an exotic exhibit, and this unnerved him and he'd returned to England, almost broke. At this point, his family were still unaware of his illegal doings, and welcomed him back. He was on his best behaviour in Wiltshire, worked on the farm, and wondered what to do next.

Then old Cousin Barraclough, of Skipton, Yorkshire, stepped in with the possibility of his managing the affairs of a certain Farmer Boone, who, if not an aristocrat, was a comfortable squire. He had never injured anybody connected with his family, so he had come to Skipton resolved to do a good, honest job.

The temptation had been too much. It was the farmer's fault. He was a fool and trusted him too readily. He'd begun small but there was no satisfaction in only cheating a man out of ten pounds here and there. The sums got bigger. And bigger. He reached for more, always just a little more, and each time he reached, he decided it would be the last time, and then he'd stop. But it gave him great satisfaction when he saw the bank trust him. He could outwit the Bank of England if he chose! Soon, his conscience stopped bothering him and he sank everything in debt, amassing wealth for himself.

The eldest Miss Boone had disliked him, she was sharp and bold and went running to her father with tales now and then, but apologies and humility had always won Mr. Boone around. Mrs. Boone used to become annoyed with him for not standing in photographs with them, but he flatly refused. He did not mind offending her.

The thought of how the Boone family was faring now forced itself upon him. He had not given them any thought since he'd left England and lived very well for several years in isolated luxury on the Mediterranean. He'd changed his name to Alexander Turnbull and passed himself off as American. He'd taken a mistress. She was a countess, very much in love with him. It suited him very well that she was married.

After some years, the money was running low and he'd had to begin again, so he moved to Gibraltar under an alias. But he'd almost been exposed there so he boarded the first ship out of port, which happened to be sailing for England. He was anxious to get away again because for his Yorkshire job no alias had been used, and he felt he was in more danger in England than anywhere else.

He remembered how he'd sent the Boones away on holidays to get them out of the way every year so he could clean up the books as best he could and cover his tracks. And then there was the last holiday—and his plan had worked perfectly. With the servants thinking he was going to Scarborough to alert Mr. Boone, he'd instead, after reaching York, turned around and gone to Southampton.

Good, clean crime was what he liked.

When Timothy Bright had returned to him in great agitation this morning, and told his story, that Miss Boone was alive and well, he'd been utterly furious. There was no time to be lost in retrieving the situation. Miss Boone still had to be got rid of. Another plan had come to his mind—they could pull it off—yes—with the help of Gladys.

Bright hadn't known how the mistaken identity had happened. He'd described Miss Boone to the assailant he'd hired, especially her hat with the bright yellow ribbon going around it and tied in a bow at the back.

CHAPTER THIRTY-EIGHT

S andra moved about the kitchen in a daze. The fact that Mr. Craven was in Whitechapel dominated her thoughts. Her pain and that of her family, returned to seize her mind. How he had made them suffer! How he had broken their family! How she'd love to find him, confront him, turn the police on him! At times, fears for Lillian broke through her thoughts. Where was she? Bright had not returned. And where was Gladys? Mrs. Lark was helping her as best she could, but Sandra was in another world, getting through her duties without even thinking of what she was doing. She wanted to get away and look for Craven herself.

Mr. Lark had known of this, and had not told her! She resented that deeply and had hardly spoken to him since, only nodding when he spoke to her, not looking at him.

A policeman had come but said it was too soon to declare anybody missing, and that they couldn't say she'd come to any harm until they found a body. As for going after Mr. Bright and arresting him—on what grounds? He couldn't be arrested because he acted odd. The prisons would be chocka-block if they did that. There was nothing he could do until there was evidence, and he went away.

Mr. Lark had implored Sandra not to go out. He went to see Mrs. Smithson, who was not too concerned for Lillian. Lillian would turn up. She was a featherhead. The cat had kittens then, had she? Well, Miss Boone was right after all. Well, she'd better feed the cat then, and let her out for a while. Would the club take a cat? She wasn't going to have four cats running around the house just to please Miss Lillian. Now, she had to go to market, so Mr. Lark had to excuse her please.

But where was Gladys?

Several people came in for lunch, which was not as good as usual, but nobody complained. The afternoon wore on as Sandra worked hard in the kitchen. She threw herself into it. It took her mind off Craven, and off Lillian. Every hour brought more worry. In late afternoon, Mr. Lark again threw on his hat and coat.

"I shall have to go to Lambeth, to visit her home. Perhaps she is there. If not, I am going to have to inform her family that she's missing." He departed in a grim mood.

As he walked along, he pondered how dreadfully it was all turning out for everybody. Lillian was missing, Bright acted suspicious, Gladys had disappeared, and Sandra was in danger. He entertained the hope, however, that Lillian was at home in Lambeth.

It plunged him into further gloom that Sandra had given him cold, unfeeling looks the entire day. She was very upset, understandably, but surely she could understand that he had not told her because it would unsettle her in what was a hopeless situation?

Mrs. Coolidge answered the door. No, she said, Lillian was not there. The news that she had not been seen all day brought concern that escalated into hysteria as Lillian's father and brothers appeared, donned caps and ran out to go to Whitechapel and scour the neighbourhood. They feared the worst.

Clement turned to make his way back also. Dejected and depressed, he wondered if any of this would have happened if he had not taken Sandra Boone into his employ. Was all the business in the world worth the dreadful turn of events?

He returned to find rumours flying about the streets, and an angry crowd of vigilantes swarming about. The word was out that a young woman was missing, and they were angry with the police for not doing enough.

A few streets away, a very relieved Mrs. Knave was loosed from her bonds.

"It's all right, Ma. They won't hurt you now. I done all they asked." Gladys turned around and glared at Timothy as she took her mother downstairs. She ushered her mother out the door. Timothy had ordered her that she was to stay with her mother for the night, and go back to work the following day. If she failed to do her part tomorrow, her mother would be kidnapped again and this time, she would be hurt. She was now terrified of Timothy Bright.

CHAPTER THIRTY-NINE

Sandra wanted to return to Witley Street for the night, but Mrs. Lark and Clement persuaded her to stay. She could have one of the empty rooms, and Mrs. Lark hurried to get bedsheets before she could object, and laid out one of her own nightgowns for her to wear.

In spite of her hard work during the day, she did not sleep. Her heart was full of so many emotions she could hardly think. As dawn crept over the sky, she began to doze, but then heard police whistles and sounds of running feet on the footpath below. No! Please God, not … not the thing they all feared!

She pulled her coat on over her nightgown and hurried downstairs. Clement had also heard and he was up also, for he stayed most nights now in the Club. He had come down in a maroon silk dressing gown. He unlocked the front doors. The crowds were growing, the situation tense, there was panic in the air.

"A body found under Witley Bridge!"

"A woman!"

"He's struck again!"

Sandra staggered a little, the blood left her head and she felt herself falling. Clement caught her, and holding her firmly about the waist, led her inside to a chair.

"It might not be Lillian," he said soothingly, though there was a sick feeling in his stomach as well.

"Oh Mr. Lark, if it is, I shall not get over it—I, who knew how silly she was—I should have warned her to be extra-vigilant ..." A tremble shook her from head to foot, causing Clement to impulsively put his arm around her shoulders in a warm, affectionate embrace as he drew her close.

"We can only be patient and wait for news," he said. Her hair was tumbled about his chest.

"Of course, of course." Sandra detached herself with tact, although his arms felt warm and strong about her. "If anything happens to her, and it should have been me—why, Mr. Lark, why did you not tell me about Mr. Craven? I would have gone to the police!"

Clement's hands dropped in a despondent gesture.

"I am truly sorry, Miss Boone! But I felt it was a hopeless situation, and looking for him would be like looking for a needle in a haystack. And without police help, for they are not interested in fraud cases when there is a murderer on the loose."

"Pardon me for saying this, Mr. Lark, but it was a matter that concerned me. I entered into your confidence by relating to you what happened to us at his hands, and you should have informed me that you had information!"

"I am very sorry, Miss Boone. If I could redo this, I would."

"What is going on?" Mrs. Lark was coming downstairs in her dressing-gown, her hair in her nightcap. Sandra, feeling embarrassed to be seen by her with her hair down, excused herself and went upstairs again. If the victim was Lillian, she would know soon.

CHAPTER FORTY

The victim was a young woman, found under a small railway bridge. Two hours later, she was identified as Miss Lillian Coolidge of Lambeth.

The club was thrown into consternation and grief when the news came out. Gladys had come in early, full of apologies for having left in a great hurry yesterday—her mother had had a bad fall, but she would be all right. Gladys appeared pale and shaken and not her usual self, so her story was accepted, and after a mild reprimand from Mrs. Lark about having run off without letting anybody know, she got to her usual work of scouring, scrubbing and preparing vegetables for the soup. The death of Lillian did not appear to affect her overmuch, Sandra thought, with great surprise—if anything, Gladys seemed preoccupied, almost absent to everybody and everything.

She felt sick to her stomach at the news. And to think it was to have been her—Clement was sure of it—it did not take her long to discover how the mix-up occurred. *The hat.* She it was who should be lying there in Whitechapel Mortuary, not poor Lillian!

Gladys had not spoken to her at all. Gladys did not even look at her. It was very odd; she did not understand.

"We have bookings for lunch and shall honour them," Clement said. "But we shall then close until Lillian's funeral is over. Gladys, you won't be needed—you may go home to your mother now, I shall send you in a cab."

"Oh, Ma is all right now," Gladys said quickly. "And I'd rather stay."

Mr. Lark and his mother decided, mid-morning, to go to Lambeth to sympathise with Lillian's family, to give them her wages and some money besides to help with funeral expenses. They donned black hats and set off. Whistler came into the kitchen. He had been very upset—he'd liked Lillian.

"Why Gladys, have you nothink to say about poor Lillian?" he asked in an exasperated way.

"What business of it is yours, whether I have things to say or not?" she snapped.

"I know you didn't get along, but surely you must—!"

"It's not any of your business, Whistler, so shut up." Gladys scurried away from him.

"Everybody takes bad news in a different way," murmured Sandra.

"I think it was mighty odd she disappeared yesterday just after Bright got here. I wasn't 'ere myself, but Guv'nor told me he looked like a ghost when he seen you, and then Gladys disappeared—I think she went on 'is account, don't you? He asked me what I thought of it, you see."

"Did he?" Sandra said quietly. "The same idea occurred to me. But I can't piece it together."

"I hear someone come in," Whistler went out to the hall.

Sandra heard her name mentioned by an officious male voice. Gladys reappeared from the scullery and stood rigid in the doorway. She appeared to breathe very quickly. What was going on? Whistler put his head in to tell her to come out, that there was policemen to see her.

They would wish, of course, to get information about Lillian's movements of the day before.

"We need to ask you a few questions," they began. "Please sit down." They indicated a seat at a table while they sat opposite. Whistler and Gladys were at the kitchen door.

They asked her questions about Lillian and her position in the household, as they put it, and whether she was a good worker, or lazy, and whether she had any young men interested in her, all routine questions, she thought.

"How did you get on with her, Miss Boone?"

"We got on fine, there was no strain at all between us. She was a good worker, quick, never lazy or anything, I never had to reprimand her and, as far as I know, she liked me as her supervisor."

To her surprise, they did not seem to believe her.

"So, you got on well?" the larger one said, doubtfully.

"And you never quarrelled?"

"Never, indeed not!"

The policemen looked at one another, then one produced a small package he had been carrying and opened it.

"Is this your property, Miss Boone?"

Sandra looked in astonishment at her cream-colored blouse, with its ruffled neck and embroidered cuffs, and it was heavily stained in dark red in the front.

"It is my blouse, yes," she said in a whisper. "Is that—blood?"

"Yes, Miss Boone. Can you tell us why there's blood on it?"

"No, I can't. I can't explain it. It was in my wardrobe, the last time I saw it. I had just washed and ironed it!"

"Miss Boone, this blouse was found wrapped around a bloody knife hidden inside the back door at your lodgings in Witley Street."

"I cannot explain it." Sandra could hardly speak.

"Did you have anything against Miss Coolidge?"

"Certainly not! I'm telling you!"

In her side vision, Sandra saw Gladys advance toward her.

"Sir, if I may be allowed to speak—" Gladys put in.

"What is your name, Miss?"

"I'm Gladys Knave and I'm kitchen maid here. Lillian was a dear friend."

Sandra stared at the blatant lie.

"You asked Miss Boone if she and Miss Coolidge—Lillian— got on well. I can tell you they did not. I heard them argue several times."

"What about?"

"I couldn't hear, what about, in fact, I had another room in the hallway. I often heard raised voices. I think, Mr. Bright— a man that was our escort home—fancied Miss Coolidge and

Miss Boone was jealous. Miss Coolidge told me she was very afeard of Miss Boone."

Sandra was almost floored with this wild accusation.

"Gladys, what nonsense that is! You know what we were arguing about, and it was never bad! We argued about whether her cat was male or female! I was trying to tell Lillian that her cat would have a family soon, and Lillian was having none of it, because she had been assured that the cat was male. Constables, that was the extent of my argument with Miss Coolidge!" Sandra wanted to laugh and cry at the same time. She was very near to tears.

"Your blouse, though, wrapped around what we believe to be the murder weapon, is evidence of your involvement, Miss Boone. Furthermore, some of Miss Coolidge's personal belongings were found in your room." They got up.

"Why would I wrap the knife up in my best blouse, when an old rag would have done just as well?" pleaded Sandra. None of this made sense!

"We are arresting you for the murder of Miss Lillian Coolidge," one constable began. The rest of their words went past her mind.

As they brought her out the door, an angry crowd had gathered and heaped abuse upon her.

"Murderess! Murderess!"

She saw a cab draw up, and Mr. Lark burst through; she heard his protest.

"Officers, you can't arrest her! She's innocent!"

As they shut the door behind her with a loud bang, she heard him shout: "Sandra! Sandra! Be brave!"

Then the mob appeared to roar even louder, and police whistles blew.

She heard no more—they were on their way.

Sandra. Sandra, be brave!

Oh Clement! Will they be successful in their evil deed, will a jury judge me to be a murderess also, and will I hang for a crime I did not do?

She wanted Clement with her, now. She needed him!

CHAPTER FORTY-ONE

Mrs. Smithson came the following morning with a black-edged envelope in her hand.

"I thought I should bring it right away," she said.

It was addressed to Miss Sandra Boone.

Clement appeared. He had a bruise on his cheek from where he had been attacked the evening before. The mob, after screaming "Murderess!" at Sandra, had then turned on him, and the police had had to rescue him and escort him into the club.

"We should take it to her," Mrs. Lark said.

"I will take it, Mother." Clement held out his hand.

"You are fond of her, aren't you, Clement?"

"I love her, Mother."

His mother sighed.

"It does not look good for her though, so prepare yourself, Clement. This Mr. Bright may well say that they used to bicker and fight also, when he used to escort them back to Witley Street."

"Mother, does anybody know where Mr. Bright lives?"

"Nobody seems to know," she replied.

Clement left his club. Thank goodness the mob were apparently now all at home sleeping, and he walked out onto the street in peace.

In Fleet Street, the London Leader office was buzzing. At the desk, he asked for Mr. Staunton. It was a long time before he appeared, in shirt sleeves, his cravat loose, and a pencil stuck behind one ear. He apologised for keeping him waiting, and immediately launched an explanation that the International Crime story was still suspended, and that he was very busy investigating the murder of Miss Coolidge.

"I have good reason to believe a link between both," Clement said. Mr. Staunton ushered him away to a more private area where he listened intently, making notes, interrupting with questions and tapping his pencil impatiently on the desk.

"We have to find this Mr. Bright." Clement said. "Nobody knows where he lives."

"Except perhaps Gladys Knave."

Clement nodded.

"You have to talk to her then," said Mr. Staunton. "I will contact my sources in the East End to see if I can find out more."

"I have to get Miss Boone out of prison. She's innocent. The evidence was a plant."

"But who planted it? Miss Knave?"

"It must have been. Perhaps someone saw her go into the house. Mrs. Smithson went to Market that morning."

"I will go there now and make enquiries. Will you come?"

Clement shook his head.

"No, I'm off to see my lawyer, and then to Miss Boone."

CHAPTER FORTY-TWO

Sandra sat alone in her small, smelly cell, cold, horrified at what had happened to her. She had been arrested for murder, and if a jury found her guilty she would be hanged.

This was a vile place. She was exhausted but had not slept. Other prisoners shouted throughout the night. One woman had bouts of hysterical laughter—every now and then it erupted in the darkness, causing her to come out in goose pimples.

Adding to her distress was that which would be endured by her family. Did the newspapers in Yorkshire report London news? She felt sick at the thought of her father opening a newspaper and seeing her name there as a murderess. The Grants would say something like they knew she was a bad one all along.

Mr. Craven had triumphed; he'd robbed her family of everything so many years ago, and now he was about to ruin them again. How had he known?

He must know Gladys. Bright and Gladys. Gladys eager to see her arrested, eager with her information to the constables. Gladys planted the evidence. Their rooms were never locked.

Keys rattled outside, she heard the lock and the door swung open.

"Visitor," said the warden.

Clement! It must be Clement. She jumped up with hope. She longed to see him! Her heart lightened.

CHAPTER FORTY-THREE

Clement observed with revulsion the old, cracked building much of which had stood in medieval times, and was probably as cold and ugly then as now. The visiting room, he thought, was deliberately chilly and unwelcoming. And he dreaded the task that was his today. The letter edged in black, in his inside pocket, seemed to press heavily on his heart.

He was sitting there for ten minutes until Miss Boone appeared. Her countenance was deathly white and she seemed cold and frail. She smiled when she saw him, but he could not smile.

"What happened your cheek?" she asked when she saw it.

"I just knocked against something." He did not say it was a human fist.

Sadly, he took out and gave her the letter which she stared at, her expression changing to one of horror and dread. She covered her eyes momentarily, then opened it.

She burst into uncontrollable sobs. Clement ached to take her in his arms but instead had to make do only with words of comfort.

"Who is it, Sandra? Who is the bad news about?"

"My mother. She's dead."

She pushed the letter across the table to him. It was a letter from her father, full of heartfelt raw emotion. Her mother had died of pneumonia. Her wasted frame had been unable to fight the infection.

"I don't like to leave you here," Clement said, distressed. "It's not right you should be here, at a time like this, and yet, I didn't want to keep the news from you for any length of time. Did I do right, Sandra? Or is it too much for you to bear all at once?"

"You did right, Clement. Be easy about that. Oh, I want so much to go to Yorkshire now, I ache to go!" she cried bitterly. "But I can't. I may never even see the light of day again."

"Now, don't take on so, Sandra. Of course you will. This whole thing will be dropped. I visited my lawyer. He'll come to see you later. He says that there are a great deal of questions to be answered, and that Gladys could provide them, if she chose."

"She does not choose, does she?"

"Sandra—you mustn't lose hope. Please listen. We will get you released, and the charges dropped. I promise." His hand flew out to meet hers. She felt his warmth and comfort there, in that very brief moment.

"No touching!" snapped the warden. "And time's up!"

As Clement left, he felt he was leaving his very heart behind him.

CHAPTER FORTY-FOUR

M r. and Mrs. Knightley received the same black-bordered envelope bearing sad news. Mr. Knightley set out without delay to fetch their son Stevie from King Edward's School. He would bring him to Hove for a week or so. On the London train, he opened the London Leader and read with astonishment that Miss Sandra Boone, a cook at Oakes Club for Gentlemen, had been arrested for the murder of between-maid Miss Lillian Coolidge. This would be a double blow to poor Stevie, and all the Boones, and indeed to themselves. He did not believe for a moment that Sandra was guilty of murder. There was some dreadful mistake.

Later, as his train sped toward Warwickshire, events in the East End were growing more complicated. Mr. Craven could look forward to his escape from England very soon. The countess was ready to rescue him in her own yacht, *La Lionne*. She suggested Brighton, for it was frequented by upper-class holidaymakers, and very few police. He had received a message that both yacht and countess were waiting for him. He'd have to go by train to Brighton, from Victoria Station.

"I'm skipping too." Bright said. "I'm going to miss it round 'ere though."

"I hope you are not intending to come with me," said Mr. Craven.

"Certainly not, I've 'ad more than I want of your company, Alfred. I wish I'd never met you. I din't know it would come to this. Getting rid of somebody, I mean. Lillian was a nice girl. I'm sorry I arranged it, now."

"Where do you intend to go?"

"If I knew, Alfred, I wouldn't even tell you. If you got caught, you'd shop me."

"And I could say the same thing for you," Craven replied.

He was nervous. If they caught up with Bright, would he spill everything to get himself spared the noose? Craven did not want to have to wonder about that, about waking in the mornings and thinking about it, worrying. As Timothy turned to pour himself a mug of water from a jug, Craven picked up a poker.

A feeling of self-revulsion swamped him as Timothy fell, but he knew he would get over it.

CHAPTER FORTY-FIVE

"Y"ou have a visitor," said the warden rather accusingly, as if two visitors in one day were too much. She stuck out her hand. There was a card in it. Sandra took it in astonishment. Who brought visiting cards into a prison?

Madame Rutskaya? Who was she?

She ran her fingers through her hair, she knew she looked dreadful. She was embarrassed to appear so dirty and untidy.

Madame Rutskaya was a small woman dressed from head to toe in brown furs, walking about rather restlessly in the stone-walled room. Sandra looked at her dumbly for a moment, until she saw the darting brown eyes light upon her at last.

"Aunt Maud!"

But Aunt Maud was not smiling.

"Sandra Boone, how did you come to this?" she demanded.

"I'm innocent," said Sandra stoutly. "I did not do anything."

"I knew, the minute I left you, that everything would fall apart. I should have stayed. I heard your papa lost the farm. What other misfortunes have befallen you besides dire poverty and an accusation of murder?"

"I got word only today, that Mamma died."

"Oh, I didn't know that. I am sorry. She was a good woman. Helpless, but good. My brother is heart-broken I suppose. Does he know you're here accused of murder?"

"I don't know."

"Somebody ought to tell him. Why did your papa lose the farm? How did it happen?"

"You tried to warn us about a Mr. Craven, or rather, a man who was a swindler. But we didn't see the letter until it was too late."

"Oh! I should never have left! You are all dunderheads."

"Another minute." interrupted the warden.

Maude cast her eyes towards her.

"Do you know who I am?" she demanded.

"No, Madame."

"First, you do not want to take my card back to Miss Boone, and now you're trying to throw me out. It won't do."

"You got married, Aunt Maud! We never knew."

"Oh, it wasn't worth mentioning. I thought I'd try matrimony, since it's so popular. I've been sorry ever since. His name is Mikhael."

Sandra suppressed a smile. *Poor Mikhael!*

"How much do they pay you?" Aunt Maud swung around and demanded of the warden.

"It's not for me to tell you that," said the woman very smartly.

"Whatever pittance you get, here's some more. Take it and leave us alone for ten minutes."

The warden looked dumbly at the five-pound note, then put it in her pocket and left.

"I'm going to get you out of here tonight." promised Maud. "I have a plan for your escape, and you can be on a ship for St. Petersburg within a day."

"No, no, Aunt Maud! I'm not going to St. Petersburg!"

"Why ever not? I have a fine house there!"

"I'm in love. I can't leave London, because I love Clement Lark, my employer."

"Oh, you are a little fool."

CHAPTER FORTY-SIX

"Gladys, I urge you to tell us everything you know," said Clement sternly. "Above all, we need to know where Timothy Bright lives. He is acquainted with a man who is very dangerous."

"I don't know anyfink! Please don't ask me!" Gladys burst into tears. They were in the hall and Mrs. Lark was sitting in on the interview, her face grim.

There was a knock on the front doors and Clement answered. It was Mr. Staunton, accompanied by a shy, drab young woman in a shawl, and one of the constables who had arrested Sandra.

"I have news," he said. "And I'm sure this will change the entire investigation. I went down to Miss Boone's lodgings, spoke to the neighbours, and got some information. One of them—Mrs. Noonan here—had something interesting to relate." He motioned to her to come forward.

"It was the day after poor Miss Lillian was murdered. I was coming back from the bakers, Colls, you know, in Lupin Lane—and saw a hansom cab draw up outside Mrs.

Smithson's. I saw Miss Gladys there get out and let herself into the 'ouse. I thought it was odd because she'd come in a cab, like, and nobody in Witley Street comes and goes in a cab! I went in home and wondered about it for a while. The cab waited about fifteen minutes and next thing she comes out and hops in again … that was funny, that. It must have cost a fortune!"

Gladys looked as if she was about to faint. Her face was the colour of chalk.

"He made me!" she cried. "He made me! Timothy Bright came to the back door of the club the morning Lillian was found and told me that he took my mother as hostage, and he'd left her with that madman Craven! Timothy stayed in the cab while I went in. He gave me the knife to wrap the blouse in. Miss Boone is innocent! She and Lillian never fought, Constable. Never!"

"Where is Mr. Bright now?" asked the Constable.

"Will I hang? Will I?"

"You will not hang, Miss Knave, if you did not murder anybody, and I'm sure the judge will take into account the fact that your mother was being held hostage while you planted evidence against an innocent person."

"He lives at 4 Dorset Place. And that Mr. Craven—he's with him."

CHAPTER FORTY-SEVEN

"Craven's gone. And now we have—this. God have mercy on his soul." Clement gestured to the lifeless body on the floor.

He felt drained when he saw that their search for Mr. Craven had been in vain. At least Glady's confession would allow Sandra out of prison. That was the most important thing. But it was very aggravating that Mr. Craven would go free.

The mood on the street was smouldering, and when another unfortunate woman was murdered in Spitalfield in the early hours of Saturday morning, it began to catch fire. Clement went again to see Sandra, to impart the good news that she would soon be free. Across the table from him, she wept a river of tears—gratitude and relief overwhelmed her. The fact that Craven had got away was disappointing, but at the end she said: "What does it matter? A few weeks ago, I didn't even know he was here, and I'm just back to where I was then, as far as he's concerned. But to think that he killed two people, in cold blood, and put me in here, for the same fate!"

When Clement returned to the club it was to find his mother anxious and upset. She handed him a letter she had received from Mrs. Smithson, delivered by a boy. It ran:

Mrs. Lark, I must tell you of a strong rumer going about that your son Clement is the Whitechapel murdrer Jack the ripper. There cud be truble tonight at the club so you must get away afore. Please do as I advise.

Whistler then came in from outside. He said the same thing —he had heard that they were coming for Mr. Lark tonight, and that they had to get away. Clement was at a loss as to how the vigilantes had fixed on him, but if they had, he was not safe where he was.

Before nightfall, Clement and his mother went to the Lark family home in Chelsea.

Early Sunday morning, he returned to Whitechapel. Before he entered Cobham Street, he saw the wisps of smoke above the rooftops and smelled the ashes. The old beams of The Oakes had gone up like tinder. It was a charred shell with half its roof collapsed. Raising his eyes, Clement saw the patterned wallpaper of his mother's room on a surviving wall. A few steps of the staircase remained. By his feet was a stretch of floor tile beside heaps of blackened debris.

He shifted some of it away with his foot, knowing it was useless, knowing that the Club, and his dreams, were gone. After standing for over three hundred years, the famous old Tudor House of Whitechapel had come to its end.

"Don't go in, sir; it's too dangerous." said a policeman. He turned and left.

CHAPTER FORTY-EIGHT

andra was released on Monday. Clement went alone in a cab to collect her. They clung together on the drive back to Chelsea. Sandra was too dazed, too relieved, too shaken, too sorrowful and too exhausted to speak; Clement was silent because no words could express how he felt. He told her that the vigilantes had burned down the club. No, he reassured her, it was not because of her, but because of him.

She was welcomed into the Larks' gracious home by Clement's mother, who rushed to attend her. A hot bath was prepared by the maid, and towels warmed. She was served tea and toast, and afterward Mrs. Lark herself tucked her into a warm bed as if she had been a child, with Clement hovering by the door, asking her if she would be all right. Sandra fell into an exhausted, dreamless sleep. It was morning before she woke. Her first thought was that her mother was dead and a great weight settled on her chest; her next was that she loved Clement, and Clement loved her, and she already felt that he was taking some of the sorrowful weight from her.

There was no hiding the attachment between Sandra and Clement that day. They walked the small garden, deep in conversation, consoling each other. Before nightfall, they knew they would be together for the rest of their lives. But it was a time of bereavement, and Clement knew that the joy of declaring their love would have to wait. Sandra wrote to her family with many tears, and did not mention her own personal feelings for Clement.

CHAPTER FORTY-NINE

Stevie was on the train hurtling south through the Sussex countryside with Mr. Knightley. He had been told the sad news of his mother's death, and though he had not seen her in many years, he remembered her well and had loved her dearly. When he had come to Hove he'd missed her dreadfully at first, though his stomach had been filled. When he got used to having good meals, he'd begun to miss his family terribly, but in time, and with love and patience, he had settled in. He liked that Sandra was near and could visit him.

Beside him, his father was staring into space. He seemed troubled and sad, lost in his own thoughts. Stevie began to examine the man opposite by staring at his reflection in the window. He had a hat pulled down over his forehead, and was absorbed in a book. But he seemed a little bit familiar. His nose, his long, thin face, his mouth. And just the way he moved his hands, everything about him was familiar. And then—the man did that odd thing with his chin that Mr. Craven in Yorkshire used to do. Stevie's eyes opened wide. He kept staring at the reflection in the window, without the man knowing he was looking at him. He said nothing. He reached into his pocket for a pencil he knew he had, a little stub, among the debris there, a marble, and some undefinable sticky things.

But what to do for paper? He had none! But he remembered that he had the letter, the sad letter written by his Yorkshire papa, in his other pocket. Carefully he took it out and, shielding it from the man opposite, he turned it over and wrote on the back of the black-edged envelope:

That man is Mr. Craven who was my papa's steward.

SURE? His father wrote, looking at him as he showed it to him. The boy nodded quietly.

A little while later his father got up and walked down the train, and Stevie knew he had gone to find the guard. Opposite, the man continued to read his book.

CHAPTER FIFTY

"I no longer think of the Oakes," Clement said to Sandra some months later as they walked hand-in-hand among the apple trees at Chelsea.

"I've noticed that. You seem at peace about it."

"And I want to live outside London. I would like us to have a little restaurant in a quiet country town. We can buy it with the insurance. What do you think, Sandra?"

"I'd like to live in the country very much. I'd like our children to run in meadows among cattle and sheep … cross streams and pick flowers and climb trees." She cast her mind back to Glendale Farm. How happy and free they had been as children!

"It is settled, then!" he declared, squeezing her hand.

CHAPTER FIFTY-ONE

I t was only twenty acres, but it was Mr. Boone's, near Heathfield in Sussex, obtained from assets recovered from the late Mr. Craven. He was very pleased to live in the country again, and to have his family together. The weather here was milder than the North.

Anna lived with Sandra and Clement. She was weak from exhaustion and poor nourishment, but the doctor said she would make a full recovery. Sandra thought the good-looking bachelor doctor was visiting more often than he actually needed … Harry, now eighteen, had moved to London. He still wanted to buy his father's land back and it drove him to work very hard. His father counselled that this should not consume his life. John joined Stevie at school in Warwickshire at the Knightleys' expense. Eliza was a lively girl, direct, sharp and stubborn, but her older sisters tempered her manner. Maud's husband had sent her back to England with a generous allowance. She kept house for her brother and clashed with Eliza and all of them from time to time, but she loved them all fiercely.

Mr. Craven had been convicted of the murder of Timothy Bright. He had repented while awaiting execution. The man who had actually carried out Lillian's murder was never found, and there hadn't been enough evidence to charge Craven with that. Gladys had been sentenced to five years. Sandra had come to understand her dilemma, forgive her, and every so often she went up to visit her in prison. She looked in on her mother—another innocent victim of Craven. When Gladys was released, she and Clement would give her a position in The New Oakes. Gladys now looked upon Sandra as an older sister.

The Coolidges would never heal completely. Lillian's grave was beautifully adorned and cared for. Sandra visited it whenever she was in Town.

In 1891, Sandra cradled her first child in her arms. She wished Mamma could see her grandson. But perhaps she could? This she was sure of—that Mamma was happy now in the way that people on earth could only look forward to. It was a happiness that nothing could take away.

* * *

THANK YOU FOR CHOOSING A PUREREAD BOOK!

We hope you enjoyed the story, and as a way to thank you for choosing PureRead we'd like to send you this free book, and other fun reader rewards...

Click here for your free copy of Whitechapel Waif
PureRead.com/victorian

Thanks again for reading.
See you soon!

LOVE VICTORIAN ROMANCE?

If you enjoyed this story why not continue straight away with other books in our PureRead Victorian Romance library?

Read them all...

Victorian Slum Girl's Dream

Poor Girl's Hope

The Lost Orphan of Cheapside

Born a Workhouse Baby

The Lowly Maid's Triumph

Poor Girl's Hope

The Victorian Millhouse Sisters

Dora's Workhouse Child

Saltwick River Orphan

Workhouse Girl and The Veiled Lady

OUR GIFT TO YOU

AS A WAY TO SAY THANK YOU WE WOULD LOVE TO SEND YOU THIS BEAUTIFUL STORY FREE OF CHARGE.

Click here for your free copy of Whitechapel Waif

PureRead.com/victorian

At PureRead we publish books you can trust. Great tales without smut or swearing, but with all of the mystery and romance you expect from a great story.

Be the first to know when we release new books, take part in our fun competitions, and get surprise free books in your inbox by signing up to our free VIP Reader list.

As a thank you you'll receive a copy of Whitechapel Waif straight away in you inbox.

Click here for your free copy of Whitechapel Waif

PureRead.com/victorian

Printed in Great Britain
by Amazon

31145893R00110